Deliverance

Enslaved, Book 2

Katie Clark

Dedication

Dedicated to Micheal, Emma, and Ashlyn, who are always just as excited as I am about my work.

Praise

Hana's journey continues in this page-turning sequel to *Vanquished*. Greater City is not what Hana hoped or expected and now she must choose between a privileged life of silence and lies or the dangerous road to truth and deliverance. A must read! ~ Donna Marie West, contributing author for *Our Little Friend* and *The Conqueror*

1

I am a Greater.

It seems like such an impossibility. Unreal. Unwanted. I may never see Dad again. Keegan. Fischer. Mom. The thought of Mom makes my throat swell and I push it away, focusing on the here and now.

I look around, taking in the enormous room in front of me.

"How do you like it, Hana?" Sindy is my own personal tour guide, but I don't feel comfortable around her yet. We met only this morning, when she arrived at my house in Middle City 3 to drag me away from my friends and family and off to Greater City.

This room is my new home, provided for me by the Greaters as I undergo training and life beyond. Apparently everyone in Greater City gets a place like this to live, but I don't see why any one person would ever need this much space.

I'm too awed to speak, so I clear my throat.

"It's fine, thank you." I have a feeling I'm going to be very lonely here. I don't know anyone in the entire city, and my training doesn't start for a week. For the hundredth time today I wonder why Frost Moon brought me here so early. He could have let me stay with Dad for an extra day or two.

Not that Dad would have wanted me to stay.

"That is the bathroom," she says, pointing to a

door near the bed, "and your food will be delivered at meal times by the food service. Of course, you can always choose to eat out, but we do ask that you message the food service in advance so they don't bring food that you won't need to eat."

"Message them?"

She nods toward a large black screen that hangs on the wall near the windows. It almost looks like a television, but it's sleeker than any TV I've ever seen. "Use the HELP comp. Do you know how to work one?"

I look at the foreign machine. "No. I've never seen one."

She glides toward it and touches a button I can't see. The screen glows to life. "The HELP comps are like the old computers, but much more streamlined. Have you ever used a computer?"

It's tempting to dislike her based on the fact she knows so little about Middle life, but I push the feeling aside and shake my head.

She frowns. "Oh. Well, you can listen to music, accept communications, watch television, or study your training sessions. Everything you study at the Training Dome will automatically be uploaded into your comp."

"Wow. Thank you." I have never watched television—Middles don't get enough electricity allowance to justify using it for things like entertainment—and I assume the communications are messages such as what I will be able to send to the food service, but listening to music might be nice.

She smiles again and nods. "I will leave you to explore it. Just remember that everything you do on this screen will be monitored."

Her words hold some sort of unspoken warning that I don't want to think about right now. It reminds me that all is not well in Greater City.

"I'll leave you to get situated," she says. "Dinner is at six o'clock. You'll be ready, I assume?" Sindy seems to be a few years older than me. Her hair is silky and long, pulled into a slick ponytail at the nape of her neck. That wouldn't be so strange, except her clothes are ripped, dirty looking, and old. Everyone in Greater City has this look about them. It must be the style.

I nod in answer to her question, and she smiles before slipping into the hall and closing the door.

The room—my room—stretches out before me. She called it an apartment. She said everyone in Greater City lives in an apartment.

A bed and dressing closet sit in one corner, and another corner has a couch and the HELP comp. The area closest to the front door has a kitchen and table. The whole place is spacious and light, with several windows that brighten the atmosphere.

I take a shaky breath and step toward the bed and dressing closet. I only have one bag of clothes. It will never fill up the closet.

But when I open the door I gasp. Clothes line the inside, clothes similar to the ones Sindy wore. Torn pants, grungy tops, and unraveling scarves. Oddly enough, they don't seem old. They have tags on them.

At least I won't stand out at dinner, or anywhere else in the city.

My bag makes a thud when it hits the bottom of the closet. I only want one thing from it—Mom's perfume. I don't remember the last time she wore it, but I can remember her by its scent. I unscrew the lid and bring it to my nose. Memories pulse through me.

A hospital room. Sunken cheeks. Weary eyes.

The nightstand has a drawer and I shove the perfume inside. Next time I will remember happy things.

The door to the bathroom is on the other side of the closet. It whooshes open when I step close and I peek inside.

It's huge! A tub big enough to lie in sits in one corner, and a mirror with lights around it hangs above the sink. The bathroom at home is barely big enough for two people to squeeze in side by side, and the shower doesn't have enough room to turn around in. This bathroom could fit four people or more.

I gaze at the tub, wondering what the hot water allowance is here. How would it feel to float in a tub of warm water?

I peek at the clock next to my bed. It's only three o'clock. Taking a bath is very tempting, and I do have a few hours to spare. As I turn back to the bathroom, something flashes. A red light—a tiny dot—coming from beneath the clock.

I frown and move toward it.

I have only ever seen flashing lights like this once, past the levy back home. But these lights aren't flying in the sky; they're blinking right here in my own room.

The clock is lightweight in my hands and the red light shines from a small, clear circle near the base. I try to press it, but it doesn't move in like a button.

Why would this be on my clock?

A shiver races down my back and I slam the clock onto the table.

Greater City has too many unknowns. It reminds me right away that I can't trust anything here. Backing away doesn't feel like a strong enough defense, so I toss a pillow on top of the clock to block it from my sight.

Out of sight, out of mind, as they used to say in the Early Days.

So far? I don't like Greater City. I don't belong here, and surely it won't be long until everyone else realizes this. What will happen then? Will Frost Moon have me demoted immediately? Will I be Middle again or go straight to Lesser?

The muscles in my shoulders tense and I fold myself onto the bed. What if I never see anyone I love ever again? Homesickness sweeps over me. Now that I'm alone, unmonitored, I allow the thoughts to come.

Where is Mom? Is she even alive?

Keegan, Jamie, Dad, Fischer. Of everyone, it seems for sure that I'll see Fischer again. I have to believe that. God led me to him. Why would he be taken away now?

Greaters are allowed to travel to the Middle cities, though. I might see the others again, at least someday. I'll ask Sindy about travel allowances tonight at dinner.

That sliver of hope relaxes me again, and I let myself fall back against a pillow.

At five o'clock I decide to get ready for dinner. The clothes in my dressing closet don't tempt me at all. In Middle City we worked hard to keep ourselves looking respectable. These clothes seem to have the opposite effect. In fact, they're exactly the kinds of clothes I would picture the Lessers wearing, because they have no allowances to buy more.

I slip into a pair of olive green pants with torn cuffs, and I choose a cream colored, cotton top. It doesn't have any holes that I can see, but it doesn't exactly look "clean."

No matter what I think of the clothes, though, I love the shoes. They're so comfortable. My feet are as light as a dust mote. I feel like I'm walking on a cloud.

I spend the rest of the hour looking in the cabinets in the kitchen area. One cabinet is stacked with dishes, and a few food items fill up the refrigerator. At least I know I won't starve before I get my food allowances.

A knock at the door sounds at exactly six o'clock.

"Wow, Sindy's punctual," I say as I move to greet her.

My own personal tour guide isn't waiting on the other side of the door, though.

Frost Moon—or Supreme Moon, as I should start calling him—stands in the hallway, smiling demurely with a bouquet of mixed flowers in his hands. "For our newest citizen," he says, holding the bouquet out to me.

Seeing him freezes me in place. I'm not ready to speak with him, to deal with whatever it is he expects of me.

Move! my mind screams.

I force myself to take the flowers and set them on the small counter behind the door, but I don't invite him in. I hope Supreme Moon never steps foot inside my apartment.

"What do you want?" I ask. I try not to sound too disrespectful, but I'm not going to pretend to be happy about seeing him.

His smile doesn't falter. "I am here to escort you to dinner."

My stomach sinks to my knees. "I'll be eating with you?"

"Of course, Hana. You're smart enough to figure out I wouldn't be here for any other reason." His voice lowers and he leans in. "You may have gathered that I'm going to be cautious with you. I won't be letting you gallivant around the city unattended, at least not yet."

I swallow hard and take in my nation's Great Supreme. His suit is impeccable, just like the last time we were together. His gray hair is professionally styled. Even his shoes shine.

"Why am I dressed this way?" I demand. "Your clothes look normal."

He shrugs. "The people need a respectable leader. They find a suit more reputable than—that. Don't you agree?"

"Yes, so why am I dressed this way?"

"You're not a leader, Hana. Not yet, anyway. Won't you join me? I have a transporter waiting." He holds out his arm.

I stare at his elbow. The last thing I want to do is go to dinner with this man. Who wants to eat with their mother's murderer?

Too bad that, once again, I don't have a choice.

I take his arm and he leads me to the elevator. Funny that I ever thought it would be exciting to ride in one. Now it appears I'll be riding in one for the rest of my life.

"How do you like your apartment?" he asks as we climb into what he calls a transporter. It's silver and sleek, shaped like something called a subway car, only much smaller. I saw a picture once, in a book from the Early Days. The door slides closed after we climb inside. "Home." At his single word, the transporter glides into the traffic on the street. He turns to me, his eyebrows raised. He is waiting for my reply.

I stare at the machine as we move through the city.

Only Supreme Moon and I sit inside.

I push my confusion aside. "Do we have to talk?"

His smile vanishes for a moment and he leans close to me. His eyes are serious, as if he's imploring me to understand the importance of his words. "I am trying very hard to help you feel at ease, Hana. You have broken the law many times, but I have faith in you. I have invested in you. So yes, we have to talk."

He leans back and his smile reappears. "So? Your room?"

He's invested in me? I don't like the way that sounds. It's going to be a very uncomfortable night.

I opt not to tell him about the blinking red light under my clock, especially since he probably knows it's there. "My room is fine," I say. Then I turn toward the window and watch the city pass us by.

I have too many questions already. How is this transport thing moving? Why doesn't it need a driver? How does it know where to go?

I hate unanswered questions, but asking anything of Supreme Moon is less than tempting. For now I will settle for not knowing.

2

Supreme Moon's home is like nothing I've ever seen. Pillars holding up an enormous porch rise to the sky. The building itself is white, and I count sixteen windows lining the front of both stories. And I thought *my* apartment was enormous.

"It's really something, isn't it?" he asks as the transporter stops at the front door.

A man taps the window and I realize my face is practically pressed against the glass. I quickly move away and he opens the door. "Welcome to the Great Supreme's residence."

I don't reply because I'm not sure if I'm supposed to, but I do let him help me out of the strange machine.

Sindy is here. She smiles at me and takes my arm. I notice right away that her clothes are different. In place of the grunge clothing she wore before, she has on some type of ball gown. It's made from blue silk or satin, or some other expensive material I've never seen. It strikes me as something Lilith Winters would wear. She would have made the perfect Greater. I wonder how my former classmate—the one who hated me— did on her Test.

I glance at my own clothes and grind my teeth. They did this to me on purpose. I was tricked into wearing these clothes so I would feel uncomfortable.

Why? If Supreme Moon hates me so much, why

did he bring me here?

"Come right this way," he says. He heads inside.

Sindy guides me up the grand steps into the mansion. Down an open hallway and to the right, we reach the dining room. I shake my head for ever thinking my apartment was grand. I was sadly mistaken. This dining room could swallow my apartment whole.

A long table with about a million chairs sits in the middle. On a far wall is some type of musical instrument. I think it's called a piano, but I've only seen one once, so I'm not sure. At another end is a window, only it doesn't lead outside. It seems connected to some sort of serving area. People in uniforms line up platters of food on a counter.

"Have a seat," Supreme Moon says. He sweeps his hand toward a padded chair. I sit, and Sindy sits beside me. "The servants will bring the meal."

Servants? I glance at the people with the food. I thought servants only existed in books. Why would anyone need a servant in real life? I can definitely serve my own food.

I sit quietly while they heap steaming food on my plate, and I can't help feeling ridiculous. There are a dozen questions I would like to ask, but asking them at this grand table can't be the right place and time. If I learned anything from Fischer, it was that some things are better discussed in private. Still, I haven't been told about allowances, curfews, or any of the other rules the Greaters follow. Maybe there's a handbook on my HELP comp.

When the servants finish, Supreme Moon takes a bite. This seems to signal that Sindy and I should eat, too, so we do.

For a few minutes there is silence, and then Sindy and Supreme Moon make idle chitchat.

I'm wondering why I'm there. I could have eaten alone in my apartment—would have rather eaten alone in my apartment.

"You must have figured out by now that I have something to discuss with you," Supreme Moon says, interrupting my thoughts.

"I had wondered, yes," I say. It's mostly true, but I hadn't realized he had an actual topic in mind.

"We need to run some tests on you," he says. His tone is easy-going and friendly, as if he's telling me about a new shirt he bought. "The tests won't hurt, but they will let us see into your mind. We do this for anyone who tests as Greater from a lower station in life."

I'm thankful my hand isn't holding a fork because I would probably drop food all over myself if it were. A second Test? "I don't understand."

"Think of the tests as dreams. You will be given medicine to help you sleep, and while you sleep you will have monitors placed on either side of your head. The monitors will read your dreams. That is all. It won't hurt, and it can do no damage."

I swallow hard. I don't see how this could possibly be a good thing, or why it's necessary. Wasn't that what the Test was for in the first place? It's the thing that told them I should be Greater. I didn't claim anything. I have nothing to prove.

I can't argue with the Great Supreme, though, so I say nothing.

"You have questions," he says.

"No questions."

He watches me quietly for a moment. Then he

goes back to eating.

The conversation is finished.

He and Sindy continue their meal, but I was done as soon as Supreme Moon mentioned the tests.

These special tests can only be for one purpose. Supreme Moon tried to get information out of me once, just by asking.

I refused to give it, and now he's going after it another way.

The people I met in Middle City 3—what if I reveal who they are? Where to find them?

I'm glad for the long sleeves of my cotton shirt because they hide my goose bumps. It seems like a lot of trouble, promoting me to Greater just to get the names of a few measly Christians.

When the meal is finished, Supreme Moon invites us into his sitting room.

"I think you'll like it here," Sindy says to me. Her smile seems genuine, but she works for Supreme Moon, so I'm not really sure how much I can trust her. "You must have some questions about the city."

Now's the time, I suppose. "I did wonder about my allowances."

Sindy pauses and glances at Supreme Moon. They both laugh. "I'm sorry, Hana," she says. "I thought you realized. Greaters get no allowances. You can have whatever you want, when you want it. Of course, that's as long as you've earned it."

"Earned it?"

"You earn things by following our rules. Doing what we want. Telling people what we instruct you to tell them. Of course, you also have to perform your work satisfactorily, or in your case, your training. As long as you're doing that, you get what you want."

There is no hiding the truth about the way things are run, not in Greater City. Back home we were coddled and lied to. Here they must tell it like it is.

"And I can use all the electricity and hot water I want?"

Sindy smiles again. "Absolutely."

I already know what I'll do as soon as I get back to my apartment. It feels too good to be true.

The night ends, and Supreme Moon stays home while Sindy rides with me back to my apartment.

"Sleep tight, Hana," she says as I climb from the transporter. "Your tests start in the morning. Be ready."

I stare for a few minutes before I nod. The morning? "OK." I hadn't expected it so soon. In spite of her wishes, I doubt I'll be getting any sleep at all.

3

"Drink this," Sindy says. We're in a huge room—Sindy calls it an auditorium—with monitors and machines lined against every wall. Above the room are windows. People stand in the windows, watching the chaos below. They're watching me, and they have been since I arrived at dawn.

Sindy hands me a small syringe of clear liquid, and my hand shakes as I take it from her. "What is it?"

She smiles an empty smile and shrugs. "Just something to help you rest during the test."

It's not really an answer at all, but it does let me know she expects me to drink it. Now.

I place the syringe against my lips and push. Bitter syrup rushes past my tongue and down my throat. A shudder grips me from the chemical taste.

I glance up at the windows when I see movement. Supreme Moon has arrived. I wait for him to look at me, but his eyes never meet mine.

He's here to see what I can tell him in my sleep, and that is all. Speaking of sleep, I can barely keep my eyes open.

"How are you feeling?" Sindy asks.

I blink. Blink. Blink.

"I'm tired."

She smiles again, but this time it's genuine. "That means the medicine is—"

I know I'm dreaming, but my brain is in such a fog

I can't make the images stop.

Mom is there.

Ms. Sewell from school is there.

The blinking lights are there.

The blinking red light under my clock is there.

Even in the mist, though, I can tell I'm being poked and prodded.

A sticky heart monitor on my left shoulder. A cold metal probe near my right ear.

Wake up!

I try several times to force my mind out of the murk, but nothing works. Everyone who's here is going to see my dreams. I saw the monitors hanging on the walls. I can only assume my thoughts are already playing on the big screens.

"She's not fully under," someone says.

After another moment, I drift further away. Deeper. Deeper. Deeper.

"Hey. It's been a long time." Fischer smiles at me and I smile back.

"I missed you," I say. I tell myself to wipe the stupid grin off my face, but Fischer's presence has me way too happy.

He glances away, his lop-sided grin in place. His brown hair has that curl on his forehead, the one I always want to brush from his eyes.

"I missed you, too," he says. "You look beautiful."

My stomach tingles and I definitely can't stop the stupid smile now. "Thank you."

I look around and see we're in the hospital, and not just any hospital, the one from Middle City 3. I turn back to Fischer excitedly. "Is she here?"

Fischer knows who I mean. His dancing eyes dull some, and his easy grin fades away. He doesn't speak, only shakes his head. "I'm sorry," he mouths.

I take a shaky breath and wrap my arms around my middle. "How can I find her?"

He puts his finger to his lips and shakes his head again.

And then I remember. He isn't real, and my thoughts aren't safe.

"When can I see you again?" I ask.

The last time I saw him was a few weeks ago. He had brushed his fingers across my cheek, protected by the darkness of my front porch. That was the night I learned Supreme Moon was sending me away from Middle City 3.

Fischer doesn't answer, but his gaze bores into me. His passion for life emanates from every part of him.

Why doesn't he speak?

I feel like I'm stuck in a swamp of dark ink that oozes through my head.

"Do you think about me?" I ask. It seems like a safer question.

His smile returns and I relax. "Always." His voice catches, and he reaches out to brush my cheek again.

I shiver.

"I have to go now," he says.

"No," I say. "I just found you."

"Keep trying."

"Keep trying what? Can't you stay?"

He shakes his head.

He isn't walking away, but for some reason he's getting farther and farther from me.

"Wait!"

My eyes are gritty and I blink rapidly to clear them.

It's only a few moments before I realize I'm awake.

Fischer is gone and I'm alone again in Greater City.

I see Sindy first. She isn't frowning, but a slight wrinkle creases the middle of her forehead.

My gaze drags to one of the doctors across the room. He huffs and begins pushing buttons on the monitors to shut them down.

"What happened?" I ask. My voice comes out dry and scratchy, and I swallow hard.

Sindy glides over with a glass of water. "You finished your test."

"So soon?" It went much too fast. I take the water and gulp it down. The desert in my throat disappears.

"You were out for nearly two hours."

How is that possible? I only spoke with Fischer for a few minutes.

If I was out that long, I could have said things I don't remember. I swing around to the big screen, like my evil doings will be posted for all to see. It's blank. Empty. I glance up at the windows, but Supreme Moon is gone. What did he hear in my thoughts?

"You did fine," Sindy says.

Her frown has smoothed away, but I can tell she's unhappy. I don't know how to interpret that. Is she unhappy because I dreamed about something incriminating? Or is she unhappy because I didn't dream about something incriminating?

She doesn't say either way, so I have to trust that if something is wrong I will find out.

Of course, if I dreamed about any of the Christians I met in Middle City 3, I will have no way of knowing.

My stomach churns and my throat erupts with hot, bitter liquid.

Sindy holds out a trash bin immediately, almost like she was expecting it.

"It's the medication that puts you to sleep," she says. "It's common. You'll feel better soon."

I feel more like it's because I may have betrayed good people, but I keep that to myself.

"Are you ready to go home?" Sindy asks.

Home? I wish. "Sure."

She helps me off the medical bed and leads me to a room where I can change back into my own clothes.

The ride home is quiet, and I'm thankful Sindy is leaving me alone with my thoughts. It gives me time to consider what Fischer meant when he said, "Keep trying." I have no idea what he was trying to tell me, but I will find out.

4

Morning light filters through the windows the next day, and my eyes adjust to the changing shade. I squint and study the windows. They are definitely changing—they're getting clearer, letting in more light, automatically.

Weird.

I take a bath as soon as I get up. The feeling of being completely engulfed in gloriously hot water is like no other joy I've ever felt before. It almost erases the horror of not knowing what I did or said—what I showed them—in my dreams. Almost.

When someone knocks on the door, I don't worry about answering. I know now it is the food service. They will leave the food in the dumbwaiter beside the front door, and I will eat it when I'm finished. The food yesterday arrived three times: once in the morning, once at noon, and once at six o'clock in the evening.

Today is my first full day in Greater City with nothing to do. My training starts in four days, and Sindy promised to come by tomorrow to take me on a tour of the training facilities. She also warned me not to go out alone. She said Supreme Moon hasn't given the approval for my total freedom, at least not yet. She assured me it would come. She promised I would enjoy the freedom that everyone in Greater City enjoys, as long as I could prove I deserve it.

But I don't really care what Supreme Moon has to

say. If I'm going to live here, then there are certain things I want to find—people who believe like I do, for starters. They will have more information about the problems I found in Middle City 3. What are the blinking lights? And is there really a secret prison?

When my fingers are wrinkly, I climb from the tub. A large, round machine is attached to the wall next to the bathroom sink. It has a curved cut-out that looks like the shape of a head. I think that if I stepped inside, it would dry my hair for me, but that seems way too strange and I'm afraid to try.

It's hard to trust anything in this place.

I stick my hand underneath it, just to see, and it blows to life. The pressure of the air pushes my hand away.

Why would I stick my head in there?

I quickly dress in my Greater-wear and towel-dry my hair.

After breakfast, I look out the windows. Transporters move like magic over the streets, and citizens come and go through doorways that lead into buildings. I don't know what goes on in any of them. Shops? Grocers? Schools?

I mess with the HELP comp, which I can't figure out at all. Besides, if they're watching me through it then I don't want it on. I glance at the pillow covering the clock. There is no way I'm taking it off, ever.

That's enough of this lonely cage. I slip quietly into the hallway of the building and glide to the elevator. In place of an ordinary button there is a plastic pad. I press it.

Not Approved flashes across the plastic screen.

I frown and lean in close.

I press it again, and this time I notice a thin red

line that moves over the pad of my thumb.

It's scanning my fingerprint!

I grind my teeth. Sindy was serious when she told me to stay in. Still, there has to be a stairway. They can't keep me locked up forever.

I hurry through the hallways, searching for a door. It sits hidden behind a huge, potted tree. Using my shoulder, I nudge the tree out of the way. The door sticks, but after a few pushes it creaks open. A dim staircase stretches down below me.

I smile and hurry to follow it.

Stairs are comforting to me. They remind me of home.

I hadn't realized how high up I was until I start to get winded. Then I remember Sindy pushing the seven button in the elevator. Butterflies erupt in my stomach but I push through them. I've never been so high in my life.

The ground greets me when I reach the bottom, and I sigh in relief. It takes me several moments to catch my breath, and then I peek out the door for guards. People walk up and down the streets en masse, but there are no guards in sight.

I slip out of the stairwell and into the daylight. Buildings rise toward the sky, but these aren't like the buildings in Middle City 3. These buildings sparkle. The windows shine, the bricks are clean, and the streets are in good repair.

Something else I notice is the road. No one walks in the middle of it, like we do in Middle City 3. Everyone scurries along the sidewalk.

A transporter glides past and then I understand. Greaters have transporters and the roads belong to them.

I fight my fascination with Greater City, but I'm afraid it's a losing battle. I've never seen anything like it. No wonder Keegan was so enamored when he wrote to me all those months ago.

HELP comps line the streets like the old road signs back home. Various citizens stand at the comps, gliding their fingers over them. I step to an empty one and tap the screen. It glows to life, and small squares dot the screen. *Movies. Directions. Transport Schedule. Training Schedule.* The list of options goes on and on. This is very different from my own HELP comp. The words and the glowing confuse me.

I tap a square and the screen changes. My own picture fills the comp. It's me staring back at myself. How is this happening?

A tiny dot in the upper right corner of the screen catches my eye. It flashes red and I can't stop the shiver that shakes me. The red dot is watching me?

Greater City is not good. I need to keep this at the front of my mind, but it's hard when so many new sights are clamoring for the space. I force my feet to move away.

The people here have healthy, round faces. Most of them smile and laugh, and their walk is relaxed instead of clipped. They don't have a care in the world.

It's the opposite of what I'm used to—people hoping to make it home before curfew, hoping to not run out of food before the end of the week, hoping to not get caught.

I pass one block, two blocks, three blocks. The Training Dome rises from the ground like a mammoth. It's a huge half circle sticking out of the ground, made entirely of shining metal. I've never seen anything like it.

Government Headquarters is painted in graceful, curving letters. A fence and gate surround the building. Obviously, only certain people are allowed inside the government buildings. I am one of them.

As I come closer, I see several smaller buildings behind the larger one. It's an entire campus. It reminds me of the campus back home, the one I crossed when I went to find Fischer the night of my promotion. I cling to this simple resemblance.

What is Fischer doing today? Working at the hospital? Helping someone else who has the mutation?

It is most likely he was sent away. Supreme Moon must know Fischer was involved in the rebellion. He seems to know everything.

My stomach drops as I realize he may not have known, not until yesterday when they watched my dreams. Where will they send him?

I take a shaky breath and turn away from the Dome, back toward my apartment. Fischer told me to keep trying. Trying for what? Looking for Mom, maybe, or spreading the gospel. I'm not sure which.

Those are the things I need to focus on, that and helping the Lessers.

My schoolgirl goal seems a thousand lifetimes ago. How can I help anyone? I don't believe in our society anymore. I don't believe in what we do. Helping the Lessers seems like wrapping a small, square bandage over a gaping, circular wound.

I reach my apartment and hurry up the stairs. My breaths come in short, burning puffs by the time I reach the top.

I quietly close the door to the stairwell and nudge the tree back in place, and then I walk casually to my own apartment. Supreme Moon thinks he can keep me locked up with a simple fingerprint scanner. He was wrong.

I turn the corner and stop, nearly tripping over my own feet. A guard waits outside my door. This one doesn't carry a small, electronic pad. He doesn't look menacing or angry. In fact, he seems respectful with his hands clasped behind his back, his shoulders loose.

He turns and sees me. "Miss Norfolk, the Great Supreme has requested a visit with you. Won't you come with me?"

5

The ride through the city is quiet. The transporter zips up and down the streets, and I watch the people as we fly by. The guard says nothing, and he doesn't even look uncomfortable.

Whatever it is, it can't be that bad. I hope.

At the capitol building, my mouth falls open as I stare toward the sky. I didn't know such tall buildings existed. It literally reaches into the clouds, and it seems to be made of a solid sheet of glass.

We climb from the transporter and head toward the building. I study the guard as we walk. He is tall, with broad shoulders and short-cropped, brown hair. He's the epitome of what a soldier would look like in any story book I ever read. He wears the brown guard uniform, the same one the guards at home wear. The only thing to set him apart is a red band of material wrapped around his right, upper sleeve. *G.C.* is embroidered on the band in black letters.

Inside the building, the guard takes us to a security desk. He speaks with the woman in charge for a moment, then leads me to what at first looks like an elevator. The shaft is glass, though, and I don't see a platform.

The guard steps in then waits for me. His eyebrows go up, like he's waiting for me but isn't sure what the holdup is.

I glance at the floor again, hoping to see something

resembling the elevator in my apartment building. Slowly, I step inside. The guard pushes a button marked *102*. I gape at the number. One hundred and two floors?

The door slides closed and a whooshing sound builds in the air. My hair begins to blow and I take a sharp breath.

The guard frowns. "You've been in a vac chamber before, haven't you?"

I shake my head spastically, my panic growing.

"Just—"

His sentence is cut off as we go shooting through the air. My stomach drops all the way to the sewers below the city, and the air moves so quickly that my eyes dry out. I close them, hoping I don't crash into something. I try to lift my hands to my face, but I can't seem to move them at all. The inertia of the flight has me frozen in place.

My guard! I peel open my eyes and glance at him. He is perfectly calm, his hands at his side, his eyes closed.

I close mine again and pray for the ride to end.

The pressure drops the moment we reach the correct floor. I'm not prepared for it, and I fall in a heap on the carpeted floor that has appeared beneath us.

The guard kneels down to help me. "Are you OK?"

"What was that thing?" I demand.

"A vac chamber. It's an easier mode of transportation. I had assumed you'd been in one before."

I shake my head furiously. "No, I just came to the city three days ago."

His eyes fill with compassion. "I'm sorry. I should

have asked. Are you OK?" He helps me to my feet and I wobble, but then I find my balance.

"I'm fine, I think. I don't understand what that thing does."

"The air moves you," he says.

I want to snap at him, but he's being too nice. Instead I press my lips closed.

"Are you ready?" he asks.

I take a shaky breath and nod. My hair is probably a mess, but I guess that's the least of my worries. He leads me down a long hallway that ends in an alcove. A waiting area sits on the left and a door to the right. The door is guarded by a woman at a desk. Her face lights up as soon as she sees us.

"Hi, Nev." She smiles at him, eagerly leaning forward.

He smiles back and steps toward her. "I was given orders to bring her to Supreme Moon."

The woman nods but makes no move to let Supreme Moon know we're here. The guard—whose name, apparently, is Nev—steps closer to the desk. They laugh and talk quietly for a few minutes. They must know each other well. By the looks of it, they also like each other well.

I turn away, not wanting to intrude on their private moment.

The view out the windows on the left is breathtaking. Literally. I move closer to the glass and glance down, which is a big mistake. I realize how far into the sky we stand, and sudden fear strikes me.

Swallowing hard, I push the idea of a long fall toward death from my mind and turn around. The guard notices me and quickly straightens up.

The woman's laughing features disappear. "You

can go on in. Supreme Moon is waiting." She presses a button and the door behind her slides open.

I glance between the two of them, but whatever friendship they share isn't meant to be shared with me.

Guard Nev leads me through the door and into Supreme Moon's office. The Great Supreme sits behind a huge desk in the center of the room. Again I am struck by how big everything in this city is. The room is mostly empty. Three walls are taken up with the glittering windows and the fourth wall with bookshelves. Two chairs sit on my side of the desk, and to the left is a small buffet table with fruits and vegetables. Dad would inspect them, if he were here.

"You may go," Supreme Moon says.

Guard Nev nods and leaves the room.

I stand in the wide, open space, staring at Supreme Moon. He wouldn't demote me, not this early. Will he revoke my allowances? I may have enjoyed my first and last hot bath.

The room is eerily silent. I watch him, letting all of my memories flow through my mind—memories of Mom being taken; memories of Dad's face, full of disappointment; memories of running for my life as Mr. Elders was killed.

"I had hoped I wouldn't be seeing you so soon," he says. He remains in his chair, his fingers poised in a triangle near his chin.

I clear my throat. "The feeling is mutual."

His serious face changes instantly, and he throws back his head and laughs. "That's why I like you, Hana. You've got spunk. Very few people have been bold enough to speak to me that way."

His words surprise me, but I work to hide it.

He watches me, waiting, and when I don't speak

he goes on. "Sindy informed you that you weren't to leave your room, I presume."

"She did."

"And yet, here we are."

He obviously wants an explanation. What to say? Implying that I'll do whatever I want doesn't seem to be the right thing.

I consider my end goal. Finding Mom and Jamie is at the top of my list, and finding Christians in this city is next. If I'm cooped up in my apartment all the time, then that will never happen. I will never learn what the blinking lights are, or see Fischer again.

Being defiant won't get Supreme Moon to give me my freedom.

"I was curious," I explain. "Greater City is very different from Middle City 3. I wanted to explore the huge buildings and see the transporters. I wanted to see the people who I've been told are so great. I just wanted to see."

He considers my words. Does he believe them? They're true, at least partially.

Emotions play across his face and it strikes me that he's not a very good liar. He doesn't believe me—so maybe I'm not a very good liar, either.

"From now on you may come and go as you please. There is no curfew in Greater City; however, there are rules that must be obeyed. You cannot leave the city without permission. Your travel allowances must be pre-approved. And I will keep my eye on you, Hana. Don't try anything foolish. You were brought here for a reason."

Again I wonder what that reason is. I get the feeling that Supreme Moon is keeping something from me—something that pertains to me, specifically.

The door behind me slides open and a guard enters. He doesn't bother waiting to be invited in. Instead he walks with clipped steps to Supreme Moon's side. He leans down and whispers into the Great Supreme's ear. Supreme Moon's nostrils flare and he nods slightly.

Something is wrong.

They talk quietly, facing away from me, but I manage to catch a few words. *Dissention* stands out to me.

Before I have time to process this, the guard leaves. Supreme Moon turns his attention back to me.

"That being said." He goes on as if we were never interrupted. "I don't trust you. You apparently have too much free time on your hands. I am arranging for your training to begin tomorrow. You will report to the Training Dome by nine o'clock in the morning."

Exploring the city will have to wait. "I understand."

"You may go now. I will not ask Guard Nev to escort you home, but see that you make it there."

I nod and turn to go, but then I pause. I glance at Supreme Moon uncertainly, weighing my next question. "Were my tests helpful to you?" I hold my breath as I wait for his answer, knowing full well that he might not tell me the truth, anyway.

His emotionless mask settles firmly into place, and he shifts away from me. "I saw a girl full of puppy love who wants nothing but to find her mother. You should be very happy to know that the tests were not helpful in the least."

6

After a terrifying ride back to ground floor in the vac chamber, it is a long and solitary walk home.

I don't mind at all. Unlike the spoiled Greaters, I am used to walking everywhere I go. The weather in Greater City is very pleasant—not too hot or too cool—and yesterday I saw a lake from my apartment windows.

Supreme Moon's words replay in my mind as I go. He knows I'm hiding something. Why isn't he more forceful with me? There was no cajoling with Jamie when she got pregnant. They took her away without a second glance. He didn't hesitate to send Mom to a Lesser hospital when her medical allowances ran out. Why is he letting me get away with so much?

Someone bumps into me, knocking my left shoulder backwards. "I'm sorry," I mutter, but he doesn't notice. He's already five feet down the path and swallowed up by the masses.

People come and go, as they always seem to be doing here. I wonder about them—do some of them have menial jobs like shop keeper or hospital janitor? If not, who does those things? In Middle City 3, being a shop keeper is a place that is respected, but many janitors are Lessers who have been shipped in to do the work.

Surely they don't bring Lessers here.

I want to know the ins and outs of this city. Every

alleyway, every nook, every cranny. That is the only way I will find answers, but looking for those things is out of the question now, with Supreme Moon watching me so closely. The best way to get what I want is to play by his rules—go to my training, walk the straight and narrow—but I won't leave it at that. There must be a way to get around the machines that seem to be watching my every move.

One thing still nags me—Fischer's message in my dream: *Keep trying.* It was only a dream. My own imagination. But it felt so real. How am I supposed to do what he says if I can't get out and search?

One of my first goals needs to be finding Christians in this city. I have to believe there are at least a few. I need someone who can tell me the things I haven't learned—I know about Jesus Christ, but I don't understand how to trust him or how to tell others about him.

Once I reach my apartment building, I slip inside and head straight for the stairwell. The jog up is just as hard as it was earlier in the day, but I know from experience that it will get easier.

At the seventh floor, I open the door as quietly as I can and step out of the stairwell. The tree can stay to the side because I think I'll be taking the stairs from now on.

"What are you doing in there?"

The voice makes me spin around, afraid of seeing another guard so soon. A girl with wide eyes stares at me. Her long, golden curls wrap around her face in a pretty cascade. She's my own age.

I consider what to say. "I like the stairs."

She frowns. "Why?"

I give a small laugh and shrug. "Just do." I glance

around, but she's alone. "Do you live here?"

"Three doors down," she says, pointing past my own door. "Technically I live with my mom, but she's always gone on business, and so I'm mostly here alone."

"I'm alone, too," I say.

"I'm Kassy."

"It's nice to meet you. I'm Hana. Maybe I'll see you later." And maybe I'll have a friend, after all.

She smiles and lets me pass. I glance at her one last time before stepping inside my apartment.

The change is immediately apparent. Pillows lay prettily on my bed, arranged exactly as they were my first day here. The clock sits on my bedside table, uncovered.

A chill races up my arms. Someone was here.

My first instinct is tossing the clock out the window and watching it smash into a million pieces, but it probably won't do any good. Supreme Moon will send something else to replace it. Next time he might not even wait until I'm gone to do it.

Paranoia ripples through me. What if he's watching me from a different angle with some other device in the room? I scan my apartment for other blinking lights, but I don't see any. I'm not foolish enough to believe that means there's nothing here, though. Can the HELP comp watch me even if I don't turn it on?

I take several deep breaths. There's nothing I can do about it right now. I force my thoughts to things I can control.

I'm hungry. I haven't eaten in hours. I dig through the food left at lunchtime. Inside a cooler I find a sandwich and an apple, and I sit at the table to eat.

After my meal I move to the window to watch the fascinating traffic.

Traffic. It's a word I only know from books. It's hard to believe there is traffic right here on the streets below me, only a few hundred miles from my own home town. What other splendors does Greater City hold that I haven't yet learned? What lies beyond the buildings I can see from my window?

The thought makes me pause.

What lies past the city's boundaries? We were taught in school about the enemies who destroyed our once-prosperous nation, but what kind of world is it today? Are there others out there? Other people who are suffering or prosperous?

Do they know about God?

Sadness wraps around me like a fog as I consider all the people out there who might be wondering about life after death like Mom was--like I was.

The evening passes slowly. I brought one book from home—the Bible Fischer gave me. I'm too afraid to bring it out of my bag, especially since I know Supreme Moon can see me.

I go to bed at exactly ten o'clock, just because old habits are hard to break.

The dreary feelings from the night have vanished by morning. I slept surprisingly well, and I climb from bed. There's no time for a long, luxurious bath. I have a purpose today; a place to be. I yank my hair into a ponytail and pull on the clothes provided for me by the Greaters. What will I find inside the Training Dome?

I'm anxious to learn, in spite of myself. It's hard to squelch the feelings of wanting to help the Lessers when I've been working toward it for years.

I jog down the stairs and hurry outside. Pigeons

peck at the ground, and they don't even skitter as I walk through their fold. I notice more today than yesterday. Shops dot the sidewalks between the big buildings. They hawk everything from flowers to shoes. If I don't get allowances, how do I buy things? Surely the shop owners don't give me anything I want just because I'm inside the store.

The Training Dome rises from the ground like the sun. The metal glimmers in the sunlight, making the world almost sparkle. I walk to the gate and stop at the guard station. "I'm here to report for training."

"Name?" The guard is eating some kind of biscuit, and he doesn't even look at me. It's doubtful that anyone ever tries to sneak inside the government training center.

"Hana Norfolk."

He punches a few buttons on his sleek HELP comp—it's nothing like the ancient computer Fischer used in Middle City 3—and then he pushes a different button. The gate swings open.

"Thank you," I say. He grunts but still doesn't look at me.

Arguably, anyone could saunter up to this gate and give my name, and they would be allowed inside.

Back home we lived in fear at every turn. The carefree attitude of the Greaters is disturbing. They don't have to worry about things like the mutation or running out of food, or anything else, apparently.

I stomp through the gate and all the way inside the dome. The interior stops me in my tracks. The entry of the building is vast and open, and even though the outside looks like opaque metal, from the inside I can see everything going on in the outside world.

Hallways and vac chambers are suspended above

me by what looks like nothing but must be some sort of suspension ropes. A huge HELP comp sits in the middle of the room, ready for anyone to find the information they seek.

To the right, another guard sits behind a desk, and this one is more adept. He asks me to scan my fingerprint for identification verification.

"You are to report to room 314. It's on the third floor."

"Thank you," I mumble.

The room number reminds me of Fischer and his dorm room. It reminds me of the faint pain I still have in my ankle from falling off of the ledge of his building the night I learned I would be promoted—the night he caressed my face.

When I reach the vac chamber, I close my eyes and take a deep breath. Who invented this thing, and why does anyone think it's a good idea? It's only three flights—I would rather walk the stairs.

I take another deep breath and step inside, then push the number three. Mimicking Guard Nev as the air starts to blow, my arms hang by my sides and I relax my shoulders.

The air shoots me upward and my breath catches.

Unlike the agonizing ride to the one hundred and second floor of Supreme Moon's building, this ride is over almost as soon as it begins. I step out of the vac chamber, brush my hair back into place, and congratulate myself for not collapsing when the floor reappeared.

A few trainees move through the halls. No one looks at me, so I hurry past them to find my room. Room 314 is the seventh door on the right, and I turn inside.

Instead of rows of desks like the school back home, this room is open. Tables with various machines on them dot the space, and only one other person occupies the room. He's an older man with a graying beard, and he smiles at me when he notices me standing in the doorway.

"You must be Hana." He stands from behind his work station and walks toward me. "I'm Professor Higgins."

"It's nice to meet you," I say. He's holding his hand out, so, obviously, he shakes.

His hand is warm and his smile is friendly as he pumps my hand up and down twice before letting go.

"Are there other students?" I glance around at the empty tables.

"Not today," he says. "I'm supposed to get in your head and find out what makes you tick."

I pause, not sure how to respond, but then he laughs.

"I just want time to learn your ideas. I hear you're one of our most promising students this year, and when I learned I would have some one-on-one time with you, I was thrilled."

I let myself smile and relax. Professor Higgins seems really nice. "That sounds great."

He moves to a stack of files on his desk and pats a chair beside him. "Great. Let's begin, shall we?"

7

The morning passes slowly as Professor Higgins tells me all I'll need to know for training and working on my HELP comp. Unfortunately, it looks like I'll have to turn the thing on. He also gives me pointers for getting along with the other trainees—the ones who are natural-born Greaters. He warns me that they won't like me very much, having tested above my station.

By midday he opens up discussion on my ideas for helping the people we call Lessers.

"We can do more with them," I say. "If Lessers weren't given the pills—if they were worked with and better trained—then we could open more factories. We could prosper the country, and grow into what we once were."

My old feelings surge to the surface. The Lessers live in a prison state at all times. They are locked away in their own cities, and they aren't given the chance to be something better. Sure, they can Test and aim for Middle, but most of them don't. Everyone knows the chances aren't that high. They need a chance. They need help. They need deliverance.

Professor Higgins nods, looking at his desk. A thick line creases his forehead. "You're absolutely right. Of course, you're not the first person to have such ideas, but you're the first student I've come across who actively wants to do something about it. Most of the trainees I get don't actually want to get their hands dirty." He glances up and smiles. "It's probably because you aren't from around here. You're used to hard work."

I don't know how to respond to his words. Most people don't say anything negative about the Greaters at all, at least not openly.

He pats my hand and sighs. "Don't worry, Hana. I mean that as a compliment. Supreme Moon wouldn't have brought you here had it not been for his belief in your abilities. My words won't get you in trouble."

Professor Higgins obviously doesn't know much about me, and possibly even less about Supreme Moon, but I do let his words calm me. Also, he seems to be just as interested as I am in helping the Lessers. It gives me hope that maybe we can really make a difference.

"Well," he says. "I have some files on the Lesser cities. We'll work through those so you can get a better idea of what actually goes on in them. Then you can begin to consider what changes you would like to see made."

He stands and groans as he massages his lower back. "I'm getting to be an old man. If you'll excuse me for a moment, I need to take care of a few things."

I smile and nod. In the few hours we've spent together, I'm happy to realize that I like the professor. He's not the average, pompous Greater—not that I've known many Greaters, only the doctors at Mom's hospital, and that was only for a few short weeks. Still, he laughs often, and he takes what I say seriously. He reminds me of Ms. Sewell from school back home.

I glance around as I wait for him to come back. We've been working at his desk, but at the table beside us sits a stack of folders. The files for the Lesser cities?

I watch the door as I move toward them. Is Mom's information in a file like this somewhere? Do they keep tabs on the Lessers?

Thinking of her as Lesser stabs my heart. She is so much more.

I lift the first file and just begin to browse through it when Professor Higgins returns. "Ah, getting started already, I see."

"Can I bring them to the desk?" I ask casually. At least he sees my behavior as normal.

"Please do."

I heft the stack into my arms and place it on Professor Higgins' desk. "How many Lesser cities are there? There are so many files."

He sighs and flips through the first one. "Too many," he says.

Too many, but how many? I glance at the stack and count eight. Eight! We were always given the impression there were only three Lesser cities—one Greater City, three Middle cities, and three Lesser cities.

"You are keener than the others," he says, watching me over the rim of his glasses. "You haven't taken a single thing I've said at face value."

I hold my breath, waiting for what he'll say next. A few months ago he wouldn't have been able to speak these words about me, but I've learned to question, to find truth for myself.

He watches me quietly, and then a slow, small smile creeps across his face. "You give me hope."

I draw back. Of anything he has said today, this surprises me the most. A dozen questions race through my mind, but I don't know him well enough to ask them. Not yet. I file the information away for later because he may be someone who can help me in the end.

"Let's get to work," he says.

The first folder is for Lesser City 8. It's located in the west; somewhere out toward what was once Kansas. This Lesser City is for those who are good at ranching. They raise cattle.

Where does the milk and meat go? Because, as far as I knew, we raised a few cattle ourselves in Middle City 3, and that's where we got our meat from. I assume every city is the same—self-sustaining.

This means the cattle of Lesser 8 don't go toward feeding the nation. Who do they profit? Surely one Greater City doesn't need all the cattle of an entire city.

Lesser cities 7 and 6 come next, and both are random textile cities. My confusion grows with every folder I come across. The people are being used to create, to grow, to build—but who is seeing the profits? Greater City must have more citizens than I knew if all of this wealth benefits them.

Lesser City 5 makes me catch my breath. It is a military base, with "un-enlisted" soldiers. At the bottom of the last page there is a single, scrawled sentence. *Internment Camp.*

Those words haunt me. What does internment mean? I don't ask Professor Higgins because I'm almost afraid to know the answer, but I have a suspicion about what is behind the walls of Lesser City 5.

He skims over that file and quickly places it to his side. I frown, getting the distinct impression he doesn't want to focus on that city.

The lower we get, and the closer to our end of the country we get, the more random the Lesser cities become. Most of them are poor, run down cities with little to offer their people. These are the ones who need my help, and these are the cities I will focus on. I scoot the folder for Lesser City 1 closer to me. They sent Mom somewhere to die. Was it here?

"Can we visit some of the cities?" The question pops out before I can talk myself out of asking. It's what I've hoped for from the beginning—working with the Lessers and visiting their cities. Isn't it what I promised Jamie? It seems like a lifetime ago.

Professor Higgins' eyebrows rise. "You want to see the Lesser cities?"

"I can read all about them on paper," I explain, "but seeing them in person will give us a much better idea of what we're dealing with."

He seems to consider my words, weighing my request with his knowledge. Finally he sighs and nods. "I will have to request permission, and I can't promise anything. I do see your point, though."

Tears burn my eyes. It's what I had hoped for, but I never imagined it would be so soon. Supreme Moon wouldn't deny my request; I have to believe that. He knows I want to find Mom—he mentioned it himself. The only reason to veto the trip would be cruelty, and he does want to put on a good front.

Professor Higgins clears his throat. "That is all we need to do today. Why don't you come back tomorrow?"

I swallow around the lump in my throat and nod. "OK. Thank you, Professor. For everything."

He smiles and pats my hand as he's done so many times today. "You are more than welcome."

I stand and start for the door, but then I realize I still clutch Lesser City 1's file to my stomach. I laugh nervously and replace it on the desk, but Professor Higgins pretends not to notice.

I hurry outside and head home. As I walk, I consider everything I saw today. There are eight Lesser cities, and there are no explanations as to why.

Why have we never been told about the extra cities?

A cool breeze blows in from the lake and a shiver races down my arms. I hug them to me and walk faster. The buildings don't sparkle anymore. The people and transporters don't fascinate me. In fact, everything seems much darker than ever before. There are lies here, lies everywhere. It reminds me that I'm here for a reason, and it probably isn't to help the Lessers.

8

Sindy waits inside my building when I return home. She lounges on a pretty blue couch in the lobby, her blond hair pulled into the same slick ponytail she usually wears. She stands when she spots me. "I've come to take you to dinner."

Great. "At the mansion?" I ask.

"No, just the two of us. Supreme Moon asked me to show you around the city. He said you were curious. I can wait while you get ready."

I force a smile and nod. Spending the evening with Sindy is about as appealing as eating with Lilith Winters back home, but it's better than eating with Supreme Moon again.

I hurry toward the stairs. Disappointment washes over me when I realize Sindy is following me to wait inside my apartment. I swerve toward the elevator instead.

She's probably coming to plant something inside my apartment that will tell her every move I make. Supreme Moon may never step foot inside my home, but he's there all the same.

"How did your training go?" she asks as we ride up.

"Fine. I like Professor Higgins."

She smiles absently.

A few days ago, I didn't know Sindy. I didn't know if I could trust her or if I liked her.

I'm pretty sure I know the answers now.

She sits on my couch while I grab clothes and rush to the bathroom. I slam the door and begin changing into fresh clothes when something hits me. The bathroom has a door. She can't see me inside this room. I quickly scan the room for any items that could be watching me, but I don't find any lenses or blinking lights.

I am free here.

My whole world opens up.

A huge smile spreads across my face. How have I never noticed this before? The prospect of going to dinner doesn't seem so disheartening now. I can sit through an entire night of torture with Sindy if it means I can come home to solace.

A few minutes later I emerge, ready to be shown around the city.

Sindy sits in the same spot, her legs crossed exactly as before. Maybe she didn't come to place spy gadgets in my apartment at all.

"Ready?" she asks.

"Sure. I'm starving." It's actually true, which is strange. I hadn't been hungry before I changed. The relief from finding a secret place must have whetted my appetite.

"Excellent," she says, leading me out the door. "I know a lovely restaurant near the lake, and then we can go to a concert. It will let you see another part of the city."

I smile but don't comment, not wanting to give away just how much I want to see more of the city. Supreme Moon may be giving me exactly what I need without even knowing it.

Sindy makes mindless conversation as the

transporter whips us through the streets. She points out buildings, which she claims are famous landmarks, and I pretend to be interested. It isn't until we get to the restaurant that I find I really am interested in something.

In the distance, across the lake, lights blink in the sky. They're dim, but they're on. It's after dark, and they dance clearly across the glistening water.

As far as I knew, Greater City's limits stopped at the lake. Who has enough electricity to light up an entire city on the other side?

"What is that place?" I ask. Regret fills me right away. I shouldn't have let her know I was interested at all.

She glances up nonchalantly then looks back to her menu. "Some sort of factory."

"They run it at night?"

"Hm," she says, still reading.

Sindy is a liar.

Hot dread creeps into my stomach. Is this the life I have to look forward to—one of open lies and deception? A life of never being able to trust anyone?

"I suggest ordering the painted salmon. It's delicious."

I do as she says, but I barely taste the food. Something is happening across the lake, and I want to know what it is.

We finish our food and head to the concert she promised. I've never been to a real concert. There were so few of them back home. The only ones I remember were small, when locals put on performances on Sundays in the park. Those were nice.

She calls the concert building an arena. The seats line up in ascending rows that seem to reach to the sky, but we sit right up front. A stage sits before us. It's filled with instruments and lights, as well as strange looking boxes. When the first musician comes on the stage and begins playing, noise comes from the boxes. Keegan's words come back to me. He had called them speakers, and he said they made everything louder.

A small smile tugs at my cheeks, in spite of myself. He saw all of this, and he enjoyed it.

Homesickness washes over me and I wrap my arms around my stomach. Where is Keegan? Is he safe? The day after I learned my Test results, he had smiled and shrugged. "It doesn't surprise me at all," he'd said.

He returned to his training two days later and I haven't heard from him since.

Tonight I watch others play the guitar and I wish it were Keegan.

The musician finishes his song and Sindy claps. People around the arena are clapping, but I don't move my hands. This man's music means nothing to me.

The man exits the stage, and another musician steps out. He arranges the seat and the speakers.

"Are you enjoying the show?" Sindy leans close to me. "Have you ever heard live music?"

What other kind of music is there? And I didn't live in the desert before I came to Greater City. I don't voice my sarcastic thoughts to her, though. I decide to treat her as I would Supreme Moon—with polite respect so that I might actually get the things I want.

"It's really good," I say.

The musician on stage begins to play and I refocus my attention.

My gaze locks onto him and my heart skips a beat.

Keegan sits on stage. He doesn't see me—he watches his guitar as he plays—but once he begins to sing, he looks out at the crowd.

My chest feels like it might explode as my heart thunders in tune with the song. He's gotten much better during his year of training. Of course, it might just be that I haven't heard him play in ages. His sweet voice washes over me, filling me with longing. I remember his hand holding mine, his eyes boring into me, telling me I was beautiful.

I just want to go home. I want to be a Middle again, with Keegan.

The song ends and the crowd claps. This time I clap, too.

If Sindy is aware of Keegan's identity, she hides it well. She continues watching the concert, but my eyes watch Keegan alone. He leaves the stage and another musician comes out.

My heart screams. Keegan is leaving! He's leaving me and I may never see him again. I have to get to him, but my mind works so fast that coming up with an excuse is impossible.

"Can we meet the musicians?" I blurt out.

Sindy glances away from the stage long enough to frown. "Why would you want to do that? They're all Middles."

I laugh humorlessly. "So was I, just last week. Can I meet them or not?"

She shrugs and turns back to the stage. "I don't see why not."

I bolt from my seat before she can change her mind.

"Hana!"

I ignore her and hurry toward an arched doorway to the left of the stage. No one stops me as I dash through it, but the hallway of doors confuses me and I stop. Keegan couldn't have made it out here and into one of these doors so fast, not when he was carrying all of his equipment. I move quickly through the hall, glancing inside open doorways.

Please let me see him, I pray. Peace fills me, and a moment later Keegan walks from behind a curtain.

"Keegan!"

He stops, his back toward me, and turns slowly. A grin spreads across his face and I run toward him. Tossing all thoughts of obeying the rules aside, I throw myself at him. He laughs and doesn't attempt to catch me, since his arms are full of equipment. A speaker jabs my ribs so hard I'm sure I'll have a bruise tomorrow, but I don't care. Tears burn my eyes and I laugh and swipe them away.

"I can't believe it's you," I say, pulling away. My whole body feels emptier when I'm not next to him.

He grins wider and shrugs. "I actually hoped to see you. I've come on this show every night for a week, just hoping you'd show up."

"What?" Gratitude bursts through me.

"Everyone in Greater City loves music. I knew you would come eventually. When did you get here?"

"Three days ago. It's been really terrible, but I get all the hot water I want."

He chuckles and shakes his head. "You shouldn't be telling a Middle that."

He's right. They haven't schooled me on all the right and wrong things to say, but I'm pretty sure one of the things I shouldn't do is tell Middles or Lessers all the allowances the Greaters get—that being unlimited ones.

"You're not a Middle to me. You're Keegan, and I'm so happy to see you."

Another musician comes from one of the doors. She glances at us curiously.

"I should put this stuff up," Keegan says, watching the girl. "I don't want to get you in trouble."

"Oh. Right. Will I see you again?"

"Can you come tomorrow?"

I smile, relief pouring through me like the warm water of a hot bath. "Yes. I'll be here."

He pauses but then rushes forward and kisses my cheek. His hot lips press into my skin and stay there for long, glorious seconds.

Keegan is kissing me.

It's my first kiss, and even though it's only on my cheek, it is more wonderful than I could ever dream. The last two months fade away and it's only Keegan and me, just like it's always been.

When he pulls away, he looks into my eyes.

Reading my reaction?

I'm too shocked to speak and all I can do is stare back.

He must like what he sees because after a second he smiles. "See you tomorrow."

"Right. See you tomorrow." But by the time I've said it, he's already gone.

9

Sitting with Professor Higgins the next morning is torture. I try to concentrate on the things he's telling me, but it's hard when all I can think about is getting to see Keegan again tonight. He's my only link to home. He is my childhood friend and the boy I was supposed to marry.

He is the boy who kissed me.

My fingers rise to the spot his lips touched, and I smile.

Professor Higgins drones on, and I force myself to put last night out of my mind.

Besides, tiny specks of guilt float in my brain. What about Fischer?

"The files for the Lesser citizens are so poorly kept that it's hard to make much sense of them. They're practically useless." Professor Higgins' words pull me from my daydreams.

"They keep a file on each Lesser?"

He looks surprised. "Absolutely. They keep a file on every citizen. It's the only way they know if one has escaped."

Escaped? Where would an escapee go? Again I consider what else is "out there."

He pats a stack of files he has pulled from his desk drawer. "I've gotten permission to show you the files so you can better determine what changes you think would benefit these people. These files are for a dozen or so Lessers who have been flagged in the system for one thing or another recently."

I drink his words in like an animal dying of thirst. These files represent Lessers who have been dealt with recently. Mom might be in one of them.

A knock comes from the door frame, and Guard Nev pops his head inside. I haven't seen him since a few days ago at the capitol building, and he doesn't even look at me today. "Excuse me, Professor Higgins. May I have a word?"

"Absolutely, Guard." Professor Higgins hurries into the hall, and my gaze flies to the stack of folders.

Mom's information might be in one of those files. My hands shoot toward the first one and I flip it open. *Derk Beetle*. I grab the next one. *Jazelle Mirror*. The third folder. *Britta Phelps*.

I sigh and am reaching for the fourth when Professor Higgins returns.

"Guard Nev will be staying with us from now on," he says. "I hope that's not a problem."

I glance at the guard, frowning slightly. "Sure," I say, but really I'm considering why Supreme Moon has sent someone to babysit me. Do other Greaters garner so much attention?

Most likely the other Greaters don't run away from their own personal tour guides to meet old friends.

"I see you've already started," Professor Higgins says, nodding to the folder in my hand.

"Just browsing." Should I let him know how interested I am in these files? How much I want to go to the Lesser cities? I have to find Mom. I need to know what happened to her, that she's OK.

A glance at Guard Nev reminds me that now is

not the time.

Professor Higgins pulls a folder toward him and begins flipping through it. He talks and I try to listen, but I want to dig through the other files first. I glance at Guard Nev and he's watching me.

I frown and he looks away. Clawing my way through the files isn't going to happen, at least not today. I sit back and take my time, trying to listen to everything Professor Higgins has to teach me.

At the end of the day, two things are apparent—the Lessers aren't given ample self-preservation skills, and their medical care is almost nonexistent. I try to ignore what that means for Mom.

"Can I take the other files home to look over them?" We didn't get past the first eight.

Professor Higgins shakes his head. "I'm afraid not. We have to return them to Records before we leave this evening. Individual files are high security."

"Oh, absolutely," I say quickly, turning around. He doesn't need to see my disappointment or the determination in my eyes that I will get my hands on those files.

We finish up for the day, and I tail Professor Higgins to the vac chamber. We take the short ride to the second floor, and he steps off and turns right.

That's all I need to remember—which way to go when I return.

Guard Nev follows me outside and then off campus. When he continues to follow me down the sidewalk, I stop. "Are you supposed to stay with me all the time?" I don't demand it. It's an honest question.

He pauses, almost like he regrets his answer. "I have to monitor your coming and going."

"Why?"

"Apparently your behavior at the music concert last night warranted investigation. Supreme Moon wasn't pleased with whatever he found."

Keegan. They don't want me seeing Keegan?

Disappointment pulses through me, and I turn on my heels before he can see the tears filling my eyes. Will they keep Keegan from playing in Greater City? If so, I won't get to see him tonight. I won't get to see him again, ever.

If they were keeping Keegan away, though, would they make Guard Nev watch me?

I cling to the hope Guard Nev's presence brings. I can see Keegan as long as I'm monitored. That's all.

"I won't intrude," he promises. His voice is sincere and kind. I believe him.

"Thank you."

We reach my building and he stays in the lobby while I jog up the stairs, but my eyes scan the bottom for a back door. Guard Nev seems sincere, but I can't have him following me when I pay a visit to the Training Dome later tonight.

In my room, I take my bag into the bathroom and close the door. It is here I can be alone to think, and right now I definitely need to think in peace. Not only do the Greaters need to watch me with machines. Now they need someone to watch me in person, too.

Dear Lord, please help me.

I pull the Bible from the hidden zipper in my bag and sit on the edge of the tub. Rubbing my hand over the still-smooth leather, I read the words *Holy Bible* inscribed on the front.

So much dissention over one book. It doesn't seem possible, and yet here I am, hiding the book in the bottom of my bag. I've been thinking hard about it, and carrying a bag in and out of the bathroom every day might be too noticeable. I need a place to store it inside the bathroom. I glance around and my eyes immediately find the hair dryer mounted to the wall. It's such a strange device that I can't imagine using it.

I peek inside and find a small ledge at the top. My Bible fits perfectly.

I toss the bag in the corner of the bathroom before getting ready for supper.

The food service brought my food right on time, and I scarf down a bowl of potato soup with bread. The soup isn't nearly as good as Mom's. I miss Dad's potatoes, too. I miss all of his fresh vegetables. I even miss watering them on days he was too busy to go out.

The windows in my apartment look out over most of Greater City. Building after building rises toward the sky. There isn't a single green patch in sight.

Is there even a place in Greater City to grow a garden?

The clock reads seven-thirty. I hurry out of my apartment and to the stairs, and I nudge the potted tree away. My feet barely make a sound as I tiptoe down the stairs. There's no reason for Guard Nev to know I ever left. I can see Keegan and then hurry to the training dome, and I'll be back before he knows I was missing.

When I reach the bottom of the stairs, I look around for a door leading anywhere other than the lobby.

The small area is dim, but I spot a door frame behind the stairs. Perfect.

The knob is rusty, so I grab hold and give it a good shove. My feet slip as the door swings open, and I tumble outside and onto the concrete.

My hands burn and I'm sure I've drawn blood.

Someone reaches down to help me up. "Thank you," I say, pulling into a standing position.

"No problem."

The voice makes me freeze and I glance up into Guard Nev's frowning face.

10

He watches me, waiting for me to speak.

Nothing comes out of my mouth as I gauge his reaction. Finally, "How did you know?"

His frown seems permanently glued in place. "I watched you take the stairs on my HELP comp." He holds up his wrist, and in place of a watch he wears a comp on a wrist band. Then he points to a small, black disk mounted on the corner of the building. "See that? It's a cam disk. Cam disks are mounted all over the city, including this building. You wouldn't have gotten more than a few steps, regardless."

"What are you going to do to me?" That is the only thing I care about right now.

His jaw moves as he grinds his teeth, and he huffs. "You have to trust me. I'm not here to get you into trouble. I'm here to keep you out of it. All you have to do is go about your business. You won't hear from me unless you have to."

So I'm stuck with him. "I'm going to another concert."

He nods and makes a sweeping motion with his hand. "After you."

I roll my eyes and hurry around him. At this rate, I'm going to miss Keegan all together.

True to his word, Guard Nev doesn't offer a word of complaint or guidance, even when I get lost walking across the city. He doesn't sit with me at the concert, either, but stands casually with a few other loiterers at the end of my row.

Three musicians play in a group first, and then a girl my own age steps up to sing. After the third act, I begin to worry that Keegan isn't coming, but then he steps onto the stage. My heart picks up speed and I can't stop my grin.

Someone follows him out and I do a double take. It can't be.

It's definitely Lilith Winters on the stage, though, and I'm shocked into silence. She got exactly what she always wanted.

Their act begins. Keegan plays guitar and Lilith sings, just like she always said would happen.

I wish I could spill mustard all over her pristine, white dress.

When the song ends, I glance at Guard Nev. He seems unaware of Keegan, and he continues watching the stage. I hurry backstage, not caring if he follows me. Keegan and I can't say anything illegal in front of Lilith anyway.

Keegan smiles at me and sets his equipment on the ground as I rush toward him. He hugs me for real this time, while Lilith gapes at us.

"I was afraid you wouldn't be here," I say.

"I told you I would come."

"I know," I say, glancing at Lilith. "I sort of got in trouble after last night, though."

"Hana?" Guard Nev asks. He marches toward us, his frown still in place.

"I realized I knew the guitar player," I explain. "And the singer. I just came to say hello."

Guard Nev isn't convinced, but he steps back and crosses his arms.

"Hi Lilith," I say.

Her frown is more mad and undignified than worried and confused. She doesn't return my greeting.

"I'm glad to see you," Keegan says. "How are you adjusting to being in Greater City?"

"I've been training," I say, careful not to say the wrong things. "It's been good. I like my professor."

"That's great. Lilith and I started playing together about two weeks ago. This is our first show together."

The words are stiff and uncomfortable. If only I could make Lilith and Guard Nev disappear then things would be so much better.

"I see you got your career working with the Lessers after all," Lilith says. It isn't a compliment.

"And you got your singing career."

"I always knew I would."

We stand in an awkward circle, the three of us from Middle City 3. If only we could replace Lilith for Jamie, things would be perfect.

The thought of Jamie sends sharp pangs through my insides.

"I better go," Keegan finally says. "It was good to see you, though." The disappointment in his eyes is evident, but I can't bring myself to be disappointed. Seeing him is enough for me, enough to keep me going.

"It was more than good," I say. "Maybe I'll see you again soon."

"Not for a few days," he says quickly. "Three days, to be exact."

I laugh a little. It's the first time I've laughed in forever, and it feels good. "Got it. Thanks."

He nods and smiles, then makes a quick retreat. Lilith scowls one last time before following him down the hallway.

"I take it he is the reason I was called to watch you," Guard Nev says.

"You seem much more interested than a normal guard would be," I snap.

My words make him frown deeper, and he shifts from foot to foot. "Can we go out now?"

I huff and move past him. I don't care to watch the rest of the show, so we head out of the arena and into the night air. It's surprisingly easy to adjust to being outside at night, but as we walk, my eyes move toward the lake, and the lights beyond. I glance at Guard Nev and he's looking across the lake as well.

"Are you a Middle?" I ask. I've never met a guard who was a Greater, only the military personnel, and even not all of them—like Mom.

"Yes," he says, peeling his gaze away from the lights and putting it back on the city in front of him.

"How long have you been in Greater City?"

"Why so interested?"

I shrug. "If I'm going to be around you so much, then I think it'd be nice to know some things about you."

He doesn't speak for several moments, and I'm not sure he's going to answer when he says, "I've been here for a year. You?"

"I just got here this week."

He doesn't ask any more questions. Apparently he doesn't care to know me better.

"I'm sorry if anything I did tonight makes your job harder." The breakout attempt and the mad dash to see Keegan might not look too good on his record.

Still he walks in silence.

I've just about decided he isn't worth befriending.

When we reach my building, he follows me up the stairs, not complaining about using them.

"I'll be here in the morning to escort you to training."

"OK. Thank you."

He stands outside my room, shifting from foot to foot again. "What city are you from?"

"Middle City 3."

"Are you Mya Norfolk's daughter?" he asks. "You have the same last name."

I hold my breath, shocked by his question. "Yes," I finally say.

"She was my instructor. You're a lot like her."

He leaves me then, and I stare after him a moment before hurrying into my room. He knew Mom, and he has just given me the best compliment I've ever had.

11

Inside my room, I hurry to the perfume hidden in the night stand drawer. The scent wisps around me like a scarf and I inhale deeply. Mom is here with me. She is brushing my hair, asking me about my day, telling me I can make a difference in this world, wishing me goodnight.

Once I pull myself together and tuck the perfume safely in the drawer, I sit at the window in my apartment and wait for Guard Nev to leave. I don't want to get him in trouble, but getting inside Records is more important to me than anything. Keeping him happy isn't worth losing Mom forever.

As I wait, I scan the room for the small disks he'd called cam disks. From corner to corner the room looks clean, but I know enough to realize that doesn't mean much. My pillow still lies atop the clock, so they can't see me through that one, but there might be more.

One hour passes, then two. Guard Nev doesn't leave the building. Maybe he really is going to sleep in my lobby.

I finally admit that going to the Training Dome will have to wait, at least for now. I lay in my bed, trying to fall asleep. It takes what feels like hours, but I finally drift into a dreamless rest.

In the morning, my eyes are grainy and heavy. I don't know what time I fell asleep because I couldn't see my clock, but I'm sure it was late.

I shower and dress in the bathroom, and then I perch on the edge of the tub and read from my Bible while my hair dries. It's something Fischer suggested I do—read every day. He said there was no better way to learn about God than to read His words.

The food service brings my breakfast and I hurry to eat. Once I'm ready, I jog down the steps and meet Guard Nev. He stands, looking fresh and clean. It's on the tip of my tongue to ask if he slept well, but he might figure out I was waiting for him to leave. No need to tip him off.

We start through the crowd of people on the sidewalks. Transporters zip past us, and the general din of the city can be described in one word: Loud.

As we walk, I can't stop myself from asking what I've wanted to know since last night. "How long did you know my mom?"

He glances at me before returning his gaze to the sidewalk in front of us. "I trained with her for two years. She was a good teacher."

"She was a good mom."

"She must be proud of you," he says softly.

She would be, yes. If she knew I was here. If she knew I had passed my Test at all. Only she doesn't, because Supreme Moon allowed her to be sent away without ever knowing what became of my future.

Anger bubbles to the surface and it takes all of my willpower to push it down.

Professor Higgins arrives at the Training Dome at the same time we do. His hair is disheveled, and he clutches a messy stack of papers to his chest. "Excuse me for being late. I didn't sleep well last night."

"It's OK," I say. "I didn't either."

He smiles in understanding, and we step into the

vac chamber together. I eye the papers in his hands, but when we start to move, they stay in place. There must be a trick to the vac chambers that I haven't mastered yet.

We stop a second later at the second floor. "I just need to grab the files we were reviewing yesterday," he explains.

"You can't carry all that by yourself. I'll help you." I step out of the chamber before he can protest, and Guard Nev hurries to catch up before the vac can suck him up.

"Why thank you," Professor Higgins says. "I can't let you into Records, but you can hold these while I go in."

"Absolutely."

We pass one door, two doors, six doors. Records is at the end of the long, curving hallway. I hadn't noticed on the third floor, but the hallways follow the curvature of the domed building.

"Here we are," Professor Higgins says. He hands me his stack and steps to the thumb scanner at the door.

I frown. I'll never be able to get past that scanner. I'll have to find another way into Records.

He reappears after a few minutes, and we finish the trek to room 314 on the third floor.

"I've been thinking about what we discussed yesterday," Professor Higgins says as we take our seats. Guard Nev takes a chair by the door. So far he's keeping his word about staying out of my way.

"The Lessers receive almost no training. The ones who make a decent life are the ones with self-motivation. Everyone else falls into despair and ends up on the pills."

"I don't understand the pills," I say. The thought of them reminds me of Ava, and I grind my teeth.

Professor Higgins frowns, his forehead scrunching up. "Yes, well, it's unlikely we can do anything about those. Better to focus on the training. The problem is, the Greaters and Middles don't want to live in the Lesser cities to train the people, and no one wants to bring the Lessers to the Middle cities to allow them to be trained."

It's a legitimate problem. I hope to visit the Lesser cities to find Mom and Jamie, and to see what I can do to help them, but would I want to live there?

No.

The realization makes me feel like a hypocrite. Like it's wrong. I push the thoughts aside.

"We need to create programs to combat this problem, then," I say. "Can the self-motivated Lessers become the teachers?"

Professor Higgins pauses in his pursuit of the file in front of him. He glances up and smiles. "You may be on to something there."

He returns to his file, but I smile and sit a little straighter. Maybe I really am cut out for this position.

"May I look at some of the other files?" I ask.

He slides the remaining files toward me and I try not to snatch them away. I flip through them, one by one, pacing myself to look more natural. When I get to the last file, I hold my breath. What are the chances it will be Mom?

Please, God.

I open it and gasp. *Ava Huckleberry*.

Professor Higgins looks up and frowns. "What is it?"

"I know her," I say before I think.

His face changes in an instant and he snatches the file away. "You aren't permitted to look at that," he says. "You mustn't see information on any person you may know." He stuffs the file inside his bag.

I wait for him to say more, to explain.

Finally, he looks back at me, his eyes worried and untrusting. He clears his throat. "I'm sorry, Hana. I can't let you see that one."

I breathe in and out. In and out. "I understand," I say, but inside I am sad.

I have lost my trust in Professor Higgins. I thought he was different—that he believed in me—but now I see he is no different from anyone else doing Supreme Moon's bidding. I may give him hope but he isn't going to give me anything in return.

I glance at Guard Nev and he's watching me, too, as usual. This time his eyes seem sad. He is a Middle. He understands what it is to know someone who is a Lesser.

The rest of the afternoon passes in mostly uncomfortable silence as we look through files and make notes. When it's time to leave, Professor Higgins smiles at me. "Enjoy your Sunday," he says. "Monday morning we will be joined by the rest of the students."

I had almost forgotten I wouldn't be alone with the professor forever, and I glance at Guard Nev. Will he continue to escort me even when the room is full of trainees?

Professor Higgins makes it clear I'm not to follow him to Records this evening, and Guard Nev and I leave.

"It must be boring to sit there all day," I say as we walk. I want to get him talking again. What does he think about Records and me seeing Ava's file?

"It's my duty," he says. His tone doesn't invite further questioning, so I let it drop.

We walk in silence for a few minutes, and my eyes look to the direction of the lake. "Will you be tailing me again tomorrow, or do you get a day off, too?"

We've reached my building now and he pauses. "I actually don't know. I guess we'll find out."

I nod and say goodnight, but I hope to see him in the morning. Tomorrow is my day off, and I know exactly how I want to spend it.

At my window, I look down over the city. Guard Nev knew Mom. If Professor Higgins isn't an ally, then maybe Guard Nev is. I have a feeling that having him on my side would make everything I want to do a whole lot easier.

12

The morning feels much later than eight o'clock when I wake up and realize the auto shutters have uncovered the windows. Dim light filters into the room and thunder rumbles in the distance. I wipe my eyes and climb from bed, then shuffle to peek at the outside world. A flash of lightning dashes across the sky as rain races toward the ground.

So much for my plans. Going out in this must be impossible.

But as I watch the streets, I notice that the rain isn't keeping anyone else inside. People come and go as usual, some with umbrellas, others climbing in or out of transporters. The city is as alive as ever. With a transporter, I could get to where I want to go.

My food arrives and I scarf it down before getting dressed. I'm about to hurry to the door when the small perfume bottle on my night stand catches my eye. I must have forgotten to put it away.

I remove the lid and inhale deeply, closing my eyes and remembering. I will see her again. I have to, if for nothing else than to say goodbye.

Maybe whatever I learn today will lead me to answers.

Guard Nev stands near the outside door, watching the people coming and going.

"I hoped you would be here," I say.

He turns, his stance as rim-rod straight as ever, his

shoulders square and his head held high. It's only his eyes that betray him. He doesn't want to be here.

My thoughts turn to the secretary woman at Supreme Moon's office. Did Guard Nev have plans?

"I'm glad it makes you happy," he says, "because this is exactly how every guard hopes to spend a day off."

I laugh. At least he isn't going to be mad all day, which is more than I could say about myself. Maybe I have a thing or two to learn from Guard Nev. "I'm sure. So, can you tell me how a person gets a transporter in Greater City?"

He frowns, his eyes narrowed. "You plan to go out in this?"

"Sure. I went out in the rain all the time back home." Slight exaggeration, but not by much. We were still required to attend school in the rain, and I did go tracking Jamie that once. That was the same day I saw the blinking red lights. The suspicions I have about my destination today aren't so far removed from those lights.

"Whatever you say. I can get us a transporter." He steps outside and raises his arm, and a transporter pulls to the curb. Guard Nev waves me out, and I rush through the deluge and hop inside.

"Where to?" he asks.

I hesitate for only a moment. "The Lake." The transporter moves away from the curb and we're off.

"How does it know where to go?" I ask. My questions about the transporters bubble to the surface. Now is my chance to get answers.

"The HELP comp." He points to the dashboard where a small screen sits. "Each transporter comes equipped with one. They take you wherever you need to go."

I lean forward and watch the street pass below us. "How does it run?"

"It's an electric current built right into the streets, and the currents charge the transporters as they ride over the grid. I found them fascinating when I first came here."

I can't deny that they fascinate me, too. The city passes in a blur. I watch the street for signs of the grid he talks about, but I can't see an electric current.

"So, what's at the lake?"

I watch his face, unsure how he'll react to my words. He's loosened up some around me, which is good. He's asked and answered questions. But does he trust me? Is he willing to risk something for my sake?

"I ate at a restaurant with Sindy the other night. I had salmon."

"The Creel," Guard Nev says with a nod. "It's a popular place among the Greater-born. I doubt they're serving food yet, though. It's early."

I take a deep breath and go out on a limb. "It's not the restaurant I'm interested in. While we were eating, I saw something across the lake. Lights in the distance. I want to see them again. I'm curious about what was over there."

Guard Nev's face shuts down as quickly as Professor Higgins' face changed yesterday. "That is nothing you need to concern yourself with."

"I only want to see."

"I can't allow you to do that, Hana. Take us back to the apartment building," he tells the transporter.

"No! I only want to see them."

He stares straight ahead, his nostrils flaring.

I sit back with a huff as the transporter turns

around. We ride a moment in silence before I can't keep the questions in any longer. "Do you know what's over there?"

Guard Nev stays silent.

I look right at him. "I think I do."

His gaze flies to me, but he quickly looks away. "You don't know anything."

"It's a prison, isn't it?"

His cheek twitches and I know my suspicions are right. I don't believe the lights are only a prison, though. I believe the prison is Lesser City 5. What other place would they call an internment camp?

Back home, Keegan and I went to a meeting with Fischer on the river bank. Other people had seen the red, flashing lights, and Keegan said he'd heard there was a prison. He said the people made clothes and food for the Greaters. Now that I know there are other Lesser cities, I'm not sure that's what the prison is for. But whatever they do there is kept secret, and I want to know why.

"I know it's there," I whisper, leaning closer to him. "There were rumors in Middle City 3, and I saw information about it in one of Professor Higgins' files the other day."

His jaw works as he grinds his teeth.

"You don't have to answer me. I know I'm right. I want to know what goes on there. How can I help the Lessers if I don't know everything about them?"

He finally looks at me, his eyes full of anger. "You won't ever be able to help the Lessers." His words hold so much venom that I pull away.

"I will help them."

"You'll send them to their deaths."

My breath catches and my heart thumps against

my chest wall. Why is he saying such terrible things to me? "Can we see the lights or not?"

He slowly shakes his head and turns away.

The ride back to the apartment building is agonizingly slow. I don't understand why he won't help me, and sitting beside him is torture. When we reach the building, he follows me to the stairs and walks up with me. "You have to be careful, Hana," he says quietly—so quietly I can barely hear him.

I turn toward him to catch everything he has to say.

"Don't look at me!" he hisses.

I quickly face forward and continue up the stairs, pretending I don't hear anything. "Aren't the Greaters allowed to do anything they want?"

"Not when it comes to military matters."

I put the pieces in place. "So the prison is a military camp?"

"Not exactly."

We reach my floor and he marches me to my door.

"Will you help me?" I ask.

"I don't see why you need to know anything about it," he says. "Someone will see us. They will turn us in."

For the first time, I realize that my actions here could still get me demoted to Lesser. I shiver.

"Are you going to turn me in?" He has a right to—I've put him in danger.

"No, but I hope you'll stop being so careless."

"I will," I say quickly. I'll say whatever he expects if it means he might help me in the future.

"Good." He doesn't wait for me to go inside before marching to the elevator and stepping inside.

I watch the doors close in front of him, any hope of

getting inside the prison vanishing away.

"Hey Hana."

Kassy's voice makes me gasp and I spin around.

"Hi." Did she hear my conversation with Guard Nev?

"Did you go out in the rain? Gosh, it's pouring out there."

I smile and shrug. She stands with her hip propped against the wall. Her shoulders are relaxed. She seems normal. Maybe she didn't hear anything about the prison. "I just wanted to ride in a transporter."

She frowns and I realize she doesn't know me, doesn't know I come from a different place.

"What have you been up to?" I ask, trying to change the subject.

"Getting ready for training. It starts tomorrow." She rolls her eyes. Obviously she isn't all that excited about it.

"You don't like what you tested for?"

"I didn't really care what occupation I got, but they stuck me with the most boring."

Her words make me sad. She's here in this place—this fascinating and luxurious place—and she isn't impressed with it at all. "What will you be training for?"

"Government work." She makes a face.

"Kassy, I'm in government. We'll be together!" Besides seeing Keegan, this is the only time I've felt excited over something in Greater City—well, besides the hot baths. It will be nice knowing someone in the class.

This seems to make her happy, too, and she smiles. "Great. Maybe we can ride to class together."

Somehow I know that telling Kassy I have to go everywhere with a guard isn't the best way to keep her as a friend. I smile and nod, not really committing or disagreeing. "I'll see you tomorrow, then."

I hurry into my apartment and find Sindy waiting on my couch. My hand flies to my mouth to hold in my gasp.

"Out for a morning drive?" she asks.

How to answer? "I wanted to ride in a transporter, because I saw others coming and going. Guard Nev went with me."

"Transporters are nice, I suppose. I came to see how your first official free day was to be spent. I understand you must have especially enjoyed the concert that we attended, because you went back."

"I knew the guitar player," I say. There is no point in trying to talk around it. They obviously know.

Her eyebrows rise and she smiles. "How lovely!"

How does one become such an adept liar? Is it years of practice, or does it come naturally?

"And are you staying in for the rest of the day?"

"I plan to, yes." I wish it weren't true.

She watches me as if she's waging whether or not I'm lying. Finally, she nods and points toward the HELP comp. "Our logs show you haven't used your comp. Is there a problem with it?"

No problem, other than the fact that they can use it to spy on me. "It's just so new to me."

"That makes sense. You may want to give it a try, though. You'll have to use it when your training officially starts in the morning. Feel free to learn it thoroughly." She waves me over and shows me again how to turn it on and get my communications and training sessions.

"You have the rest of the day to work on it."

"Absolutely." I tap a few icons just to show her I mean it. Is she going to stay with me all day?

But she doesn't. I thank her for her help and she leaves soundlessly, leaves me to get myself caught in something illegal, no doubt.

13

I tap the *Receive Communications* box and the screen changes. It shows pictures of various people and beside each picture are messages. Sindy has sent me several—one for every day I've been here. She knows I haven't looked at the HELP comp even once, so why continue sending messages?

The most recent message was this morning. *I will be arriving at your apartment around nine o'clock. See you then.*

It's pleasant enough, but there is no thought for whether or not I had other plans.

It doesn't matter—I have to do what they say if I want to eat their food and use their transporters. Does everyone in Greater City live this way, with daily check-ins and constant monitoring? I would have to say no because most of them are happy to follow the rules, but Supreme Moon knows I am not.

There is a generic welcome message from the Great Supreme himself, and also an introductory message from Professor Higgins. Other names are listed in his message, and when I look through them, I realize it must be a class message he sent to all the trainees. Nothing else interests me, and I delete them all. Now to figure out how to get back to the main screen.

I tap an "x" and the screen goes black.

"No!" I quickly tap the screen again, and the

picture reappears. This time I tap the *Watch Movies* box, and I spend the next two hours fascinated by the people on the screen. This must have been what Keegan talked about in his letters—a play on a large screen. Fascinating.

The Greaters have all this, and yet they can't print new books?

Chalk that up to another lie. They don't want to waste their resources on printing new books for the Middles and Lessers. I'll add books to my list of things that could help the Lessers.

When the movie finishes, I mess around with the screen until it returns to the main menu, then I go to the music link. When I see what's there, I realize I should have tried it first.

I find what I'm looking for immediately. *Local Concerts*. I tap the box and a list of upcoming concerts appears. Not only does it show the concerts, it also shows who will play them. I tap that list first, and I see there is a concert tonight. Keegan will be there.

I told Guard Nev and Sindy that I would be staying in, but my plans have changed.

I back out of that screen and go to the list of recent concerts. After I find Keegan's name, I tap *play*, and the sound of Keegan's playing fills my apartment.

My breath catches and my chest tightens as tears fill my eyes. I can hear him whenever I want to hear him. He can serenade me and comfort me, even when Supreme Moon keeps me from him, even when I am alone.

I am with you.

The thought comes from nowhere, but I don't have to question what it means. I am not alone, not ever.

Suddenly, the past few weeks seem way too heavy

a burden to bear. Being promoted to Greater, leaving my family and friends, starting over in a new city, and being kept prisoner to Supreme Moon is overwhelming. I miss Mom and Jamie. I miss Keegan and home. I miss Fischer.

Again I wonder where Fischer is. What has become of him? It's something I don't know if I'll ever find the answer to.

Darkness comes much earlier than usual, due to the rain. Getting across town shouldn't be a problem, though, not if I have a transporter. Guard Nev stands at the stairs when I reach the ground floor. "Going somewhere?"

"I want to see my friend again. He's playing at the concert arena." I've come to the realization that being upfront with Guard Nev is the best way to get what I want with him.

Questions are written all over his face, but he doesn't ask them. Apparently, we are back to that. "I'll call the transporter." He steps into the rain and gets a transporter to stop for the second time today, and he helps me climb inside. Then he tells the HELP comp where to go.

We pull away and ride in silence, but I can practically feel the tension rising from every part of him. It's been hours. Shouldn't he be over what happened this morning?

The longer we ride, though, the more I see it from his point of view. He views seeing Keegan as something I shouldn't be doing. As something illegal.

Am I doing something illegal with Keegan? I don't see how. "He's only a friend," I try to explain. "He lived next to me in Middle City 3 my whole life. He reminds me of home."

Guard Nev finally looks at me. "You don't owe me an explanation." He turns away and I sigh.

I have lost his trust.

The concert hall isn't as crowded as it has been. Most people must be staying out of the cold, damp night. We shuffle to the front and wait for the first act to begin. My knee bounces up and down as I tap my foot in anticipation. I force the knee to be still. Since when do I have nervous ticks?

I don't have to wait long. Keegan is the first one out, and he drags a long cord with him. He attaches it to the speaker.

"This song is for the girl I've always loved," he says into the microphone.

I glance at myself to make sure I haven't melted into a puddle right on the arena floor. My gaze finds Guard Nev. He's frowning, his eyes narrowed.

A queasy feeling spreads through my stomach, and I look away. I don't like the look on his face, but I won't focus on that. Instead, I'll focus on the beautiful song coming from Keegan's mouth, a song for me.

Keegan finds me in the crowd and smiles.

My heart explodes.

For today, for right now, Fischer doesn't exist. The fact that Keegan refuses to believe in God doesn't exist. Supreme Moon doesn't exist and Mom's mutation doesn't exist. Only Keegan exists.

And, for now, that is enough.

14

Keegan makes eye contact with me and nods toward the back as soon as he finishes his song. I hurry backstage, Guard Nev close behind. This time Keegan is alone, and he doesn't hesitate to lead us into one of the rooms behind the closed doors in the hallway.

"Lilith isn't with you tonight?"

"No, she was assigned to a different show in Middle City 1."

I don't have to say how glad I am—Keegan knows.

"She isn't as bad as you think," he says. My face must show my disbelief because he bursts into laughter. "I know she was pretty bad, but she's OK to be around."

Keegan shouldn't be hanging out with Lilith. He should be with me. "I don't want to talk about her. When do you get to go home again?"

His laughter fades away and he takes my hand. "I'll look after your dad. He'll be OK."

I swallow around the lump in my throat and nod. He knew what I was getting after. Of course he knew. "Thanks."

He glances at Guard Nev. "Is he always with you?"

I smile at Guard Nev, who magnanimously ignores us. "I guess so. Supreme Moon doesn't trust me."

"I can't imagine why."

I laugh, even though it's technically not funny, my committing crimes and all. Keegan is like a refreshing breeze after being in a stifling hot school building all day. My heart is light when I'm with him.

"I'm surprised they're even allowing you into the city once they figured out who you were."

He shrugs, looking again at Guard Nev. "They questioned me when I returned to my training, but they figured out pretty quickly that I didn't know anything about what you'd been up to. It wasn't hard to convince them, since I didn't live in the same city as you."

Keegan must be good at skirting the truth.

I want to say more—I almost do—but I can't. After Guard Nev's reaction today about the prison, I know he won't like me talking to Keegan about the lights across the lake. "I've been working at the Training Dome with a man named Professor Higgins," I say instead. "We've been discussing methods to help the Lessers. We're close to some really great ideas."

Keegan grins. "That doesn't surprise me at all. I knew you could do it."

I shrug and look at my lap. "I'm more motivated now than I ever was before."

"Will you get to travel to their cities?"

I'm not sure if he means the Lessers themselves, or Mom and Jamie, but I nod. "Professor Higgins said he would ask permission to take a few trips to the Lesser cities to see if I can gain any other ideas about how to help them."

"You mom would be so proud of you," Keegan says. "And Jamie would be, too."

"Thanks."

We sit quietly, infinitely happy just to be together.

God must have known I needed an advocate.

"Do you get letters here?" Keegan asks, but he doesn't meet my eye, and it hits me that he's not asking for himself. He wants to know if Fischer has contacted me.

"I haven't heard from anyone," I say. "I don't even know if I'm allowed."

"You're a Greater, Hana. If you want mail, I'm sure you can get it. I'll write you."

My spirit soars and I can't keep the smile from my face. "I would love that." It's too bad he isn't a Greater, too, and we could send communications to each other over the HELP comp.

He glances again at Guard Nev.

Both of us are aching to speak more about the things that happened a few weeks ago in Middle City 3.

"You'll write me back?" Keegan asks.

"Of course," I say quickly. I just hope my letters aren't screened.

"Good. I'll look forward to it."

A different guard sticks his head inside the room. He pauses when he sees Guard Nev and me, but he speaks to Keegan. "Time to load up."

Keegan stands and I don't care what Guard Nev says. I hug Keegan with all my might, resting my cheek against his warm chest.

"You'll find her," Keegan whispers into my hair.

I take a deep, shaky breath and smile. "I'll write you soon."

"I'll see you soon," he says. "How did you know I would be here?"

I can't tell him about the HELP comps, so I shrug. "I found a concert schedule." I hug him one last time.

"I miss you."

He swallows and his jaw works. "I miss you, too." Then he picks up his gear and disappears out the door.

Guard Nev doesn't speak as we move to the outside of the concert hall. The rain has almost stopped, and a transporter pulls to the curb to drive us home. Once we're on our way, though, he leans close to me. "You need to forget about him."

I frown. Maybe he will turn me in, after all. Maybe Keegan and I were too obvious with our talk of letters.

"Middles aren't permitted to marry Greaters."

His words aren't what I was expecting at all. "What?"

"Middles tested as Middles. They cannot be permitted to move to Greater City when they haven't tested for that," he says. "I saw the way you looked at each other. You might as well forget it."

I shift uncomfortably, a headache starting in my temples. "I don't know what you're talking about."

"I think you do. Trust me, they won't allow it."

Marrying Keegan—or anyone else right now—is the farthest thing from my mind. Anyway, how does he know these things? My first memory of him flashes through my mind. Him and the secretary at Supreme Moon's office?

He's allowed me into a piece of his life. That's trust, and that is good.

Still, his words bother me. A relationship between Keegan and I wouldn't work anymore, anyway. I couldn't commit to a life with him when our beliefs are so different. I read it in the Bible—can two walk together except they be agreed?

The thought bothers me for the rest of the drive. Should I not be seeing Keegan? Why would God bring us back together if I shouldn't spend time with him?

When we reach my building, I hurry to the stairs without a goodnight. I don't want to see the pity in Guard Nev's eyes. Once I'm in my apartment, I realize I have no paper to write a letter. I look to the ceiling and sigh. I do not want to go back to Guard Nev with a favor. I dig through drawers, searching for anything I can write with. The more I look, the more I realize I need to shop. I've only been here a week, but I'm seriously lacking in just about everything.

I finally find something usable behind the HELP comp. Papers are stacked inside a small machine on the side of the comp. I pull out several sheets and write my letter. I tell Keegan about the lights, the extra Lesser cities, and the prison/military training camp. He'll know what to do with the information, if anything.

My hand lingers at the end of the page. I want to tell him how happy I am to find him, how much I love him. Something stops me, though. Is it Guard Nev's words or something deeper?

I quickly sign my name and fold the letter. There will be time to sort out my feelings and beliefs later. I hope.

15

It takes some searching the next morning, but Guard Nev helps me find a mail station to send Keegan's letter. After that, we hurry to the Training Dome. The students are scheduled to arrive at nine o'clock in the morning, but I want to get there early to gauge Professor Higgins' behavior toward me after our uncomfortable moments on Saturday when I saw Ava's file. If he doesn't trust me anymore, then I'll never be able to get him to help me find Mom.

Guard Nev walks in silence, his long legs hard to keep up with.

"I thought you might be pulled from tailing me once classes started," I say as we walk.

"No word on that yet."

He doesn't expound or even look at me, so we finish our walk in silence. Professor Higgins is setting up work stations around the room, and he waves as we enter. "You're early."

"I don't like being late," I say. This is true. In Middle City 3, tardiness wasn't permitted.

"A good habit to be in. Today will be a bit different than what we've been doing. The new students are all Greater-born. They won't be as passionate about their field of study as you are, and we'll have to start more slowly. I hope to get back to focusing on the Lessers soon."

His words bring a sting of disappointment, but I

realize this is a government class. There are other stations of government besides Lesser care.

He's acting normal toward me, though. It's a bigger relief than I thought it would be. He might help me find Mom, after all.

The other students trickle in as it gets closer to nine o'clock. I count ten, twenty, thirty students.

I remember the career fair just before the Test back home. I only saw one other student speaking with the government rep. I guess I expected it to be the same in Greater City. I was wrong.

Kassy comes in and her gaze searches me out immediately. "I waited for you this morning before I realized you were already gone."

I smile and shrug. "Sorry. But I'm so glad to see a friendly face."

She shrugs. "I know a few of the others, but we weren't friends. My boyfriend tested as a doctor." Her face shows me how un-happy this makes her. Suddenly she frowns. "Wait, you don't know anyone else in the room?"

I pause, not sure how to explain it to her. She's going to find out soon enough, but the thought of her not liking me because I was a Middle hurts me. "I'm not from Greater City."

Her frown deepens as she considers what I said. "You were a Middle?"

I nod, swallowing around the swelling in my throat. She's going to hate me.

"Wow. I've never met a Middle before."

She doesn't care? I laugh as relief floods through me.

Professor Higgins welcomes everyone, and the day starts off slowly. By the end of class, we've barely made any progress at all, except for Professor Higgins explaining the basic concepts of government to the other students. Didn't they take economics in school?

They are my own age, but I feel eons ahead of them. Why didn't I feel this way about the students back home? I look around the room, searching the faces of these students. They haven't seen the things I've seen, or worried about the things I've worried about.

If I feel older it's because I am, at least emotionally.

The week passes slowly. I check for mail from Keegan each day, but I'm always disappointed. I don't have to worry that he won't write like I did a few months ago—now I worry they will censor our letters.

With each passing day, I feel more sorrow for the Greaters than ever before. These students are less prepared for life than I could have imagined. Maybe those raised in the Middle cities are the luckiest of all.

The only bright spot in training is spending time with Kassy. She misses her boyfriend and hasn't seen him in weeks. Doctors train on the other side of the city, and they have to travel to Middle City 3 for various medical classes.

Every time she talks about my home city, my stomach clenches and I grind my teeth. I want to go there so badly it actually makes my body ache.

On Saturday, relief pours through me when Professor Higgins announces the topic for the day—the Lesser cities.

"They're a lost cause," one of the students says. His name is Berry, and he's the shortest boy I've ever seen. His face is thick, to match his body, but he looks like solid muscle.

Berry wants to specialize in city expansion—

apparently the Greaters are allowed to have more than two children, and the city is growing.

"Do you even know anything about them?" I ask. I work to control my voice so I'm not accusing him of anything, but he sneers anyway.

"Do I need to? They are Lesser for a reason—either they tested that way, or they broke the law."

"Some of them never Test because they assume it won't help them, others don't want to leave their homes." I learned this from Fischer who had friends who wouldn't Test for this very reason. "It doesn't mean they deserve less."

Berry narrows his eyes. "You aren't from Greater City are you? You're the Middle who was promoted. I heard my father talking about you." He turns away. "As far as I'm concerned, you don't belong here, either."

His words sting at first, but then I realize they're absolutely true. I don't belong here, but since I am here I will do my best to finish the job I came to do.

"That's enough of that," Professor Higgins says with a frown. He moves on, changing the subject. "I've arranged a trip to visit Lesser City 1 next week. I want you to prepare yourselves for what you will see. Some of you may work on staff with Supreme Moon someday—you will need to understand the inner workings of the other cities."

He goes on for a few minutes, but I barely hear him. The Lesser cities! The travel was approved. I clasp my hands together in my lap when I realize they're shaking, and I want to throw myself at Professor Higgins and hug him. He's helping me after all, even if I'm not entirely trustworthy to him.

A girl with black hair and skin raises her hand.

Meely is her name. "Will we also visit the Middle cities?"

I hold my breath, waiting for the answer. I hadn't even considered that we might visit my home city.

"We likely will, yes, though I won't be scheduling those trips for a few months."

"I still say it's a waste of our time," Berry says. "The programs we have in place for them are fine the way they are."

"Don't you think all people deserve a chance? Don't you think they deserve to aim for something higher?"

Berry smirks. "What's higher than Greater? They didn't shoot for that."

I grip the table so hard my knuckles turn white. "If you think there is nothing higher than Greater, than you are a fool." As soon as the words are out I freeze. Stupid, stupid! I glance around, but the other students don't seem to realize what I said.

Professor Higgins watches me with an odd expression, though, and Guard Nev is scowling at me—which isn't so unusual.

Berry rolls his eyes and turns away, and the other students ignore me as if they agree with Berry's words from earlier. I don't belong here, and my opinion doesn't matter. Professor Higgins' warning from our first day runs through my mind—very few people want to help the Lessers, and even fewer want to get their hands dirty doing it.

I don't allow their opinions to bother me. They're partly right, and besides, I'm not here to please them.

Class lets out for the week, and I'm relieved to have a day off tomorrow. I already know that Keegan won't be in town tonight or tomorrow—he hasn't come all week—so I have two other options. I can try to get into Records, or I can figure out a way to get to the lake and learn what I can about the lights. My only obstacle is Guard Nev. He'll never let me do either one of them, so I have to find a way around him.

Professor Higgins stops me once the other students leave. "What did you mean when you said there was something bigger than the Greaters?" His words are soft and curious, not accusing.

"Nothing," I say immediately, but guilt washes over me. What if Fischer had shut me out and refused to share the truth? What if Mom had never learned about Jesus Christ?

I look down and shuffle my feet, then I glance toward the door. Guard Nev faces the open hallway, and he seems to be talking to someone. I sigh. "I meant a God."

Professor Higgins doesn't gasp or explode with anger. His reaction surprises me, because he smiles. He pats my shoulder. "That's what I suspected. I will see you on Monday."

After I get over the shock of it, I hurry to Guard Nev and we leave.

Was Professor Higgins happy? If so, there is only one explanation. He knows God. He is a Christian. If this is true then there are Christians in Greater City. My heart speeds up and I match my steps to the rhythm. How can I find them? The possibility seems too good to be true.

We reach my apartment and the door man hands me an envelope. "This came from the post, Miss Norfolk."

I take the letter and smile. He has just made my day.

16

I hurry for the stairs but Guard Nev stops me by the arm. He's never come close to touching me, let alone grabbing me.

"You don't know what you're doing."

"What are you talking about?" I jerk away from him. We've learned to get along well over the last weeks, and I'm not sure about his sudden threatening appearance. Is he upset about the letter?

"I'm talking about what you said in training today. You may think you can spread your beliefs and help the Lessers, but you're doing nothing but sending them to die. You don't know the things I know."

He follows me into the stairwell and nods slightly toward one corner. A smooth, silver disk is mounted on the wall—a cam disk.

I position myself in front of him so the cam disk can't pick up my face and can only see part of his. "Then tell me the things you know."

He shakes his head. "I am under orders."

"Orders from a liar. He uses us all for the gain of himself."

"You don't know what you're saying."

"So you think Supreme Moon is a fair leader?" I ask in disbelief. He's making my anger boil to the top.

"Lower your voice," he says. "And of course not."

We're getting winded as we near my floor. "Supreme Moon has goals you know nothing about, and digging around for them will get you killed. If you think there's some kind of higher purpose in life, well, you're going to do nothing but start the war sooner."

The war?

Shivers race up my arm and I swallow my nerves. If we're at war it is a well-kept secret.

We don't speak anymore, and he watches me until I make it inside my room. My gaze moves to the windows, and I search the horizon. What else is out there?

Food sits in a bag in my dumb waiter, and my HELP comp glows blue, waiting patiently for me to step over and play with it.

Those things can wait, though. For now, I have Keegan's letter. I act nonchalant as I slip off my shoes and head to the bathroom, but inside I rip the envelope open.

Dear Hana,

Seeing you in Greater City is like nothing I ever hoped for. Honestly? I thought I would never see you again. Learning you are still you, and that you're still as passionate as ever about your goals, makes me smile.

I have no idea if we can ever be together, or if you even want to be, but I will try everything I can to make it happen.

In answer to your questions, I think you're on the right track. I will do everything I can to find answers, but that won't be much. Kids talk—but it's only kids. You know more than us all, I think. Also, I will do what you say. I will think about it. That's all I can promise there.

I love you, Hana. I always have and I always will.

With love,

Keegan

I stare at the letter as a tear drops off my chin. He

loves me. How am I supposed to refuse that? I want to condemn myself for the thought, but I'll probably never see Fischer again, and Keegan promised to think about the things we heard at the river-side meeting in Middle City 3. He promised to consider salvation. That's a start.

The letter is precious to me. I can't bear to tear it up or burn it or throw it away. Instead I pull my Bible from the hair dryer and slip the letter inside. It will be my safe-keeping place.

Once my face is sufficiently tear free, I exit the room to find something to eat, then I move to the HELP comp. I have one communication, from Sindy. *Coming by in the morning. I'll see you at ten o'clock for brunch.*

Spending the day with Sindy is the last thing I want to do. I don't want to spend the day with anyone, if I can help it. If only all these people would leave me alone I could get some answers.

I delete the communication with a vengeance then settle in to eat. My one day off will be ruined now, for sure.

It's sometime after the auto shutters close that there's a knock at my door. I hurry to answer it, anxious to see who would be coming after dark. Kassy stands on the other side, smiling shyly. "I hope I'm not interrupting you. Can I come in?"

"It's OK. Come in." I open the door wide. She doesn't seem upset or in trouble, and I let my guard down.

"You're probably wondering why I would come over so late."

I smile and shrug. "I don't mind."

"I'm just so bored," she says. "It's always the same

old thing. My mom is gone and my friends are busy. Why did they have to separate us all?" The frustration in her voice comes through loud and clear, but it's her last sentence that gets me.

"Separate you?"

She rolls her eyes and plops onto the couch. "They said we needed to separate—that we were too close. They sent my best friend to train for the military, and you already know about my boyfriend. It's like they wanted to make sure we could never see each other again."

She is so utterly clueless that I'm not sure how to respond, but one thing is clear to me.

Kassy has answers. She may not even know that she has answers, but they're somewhere inside her brain.

"Why would they do that?" I cast a glance behind me to make sure the clock is covered, but they can probably hear us somehow.

She waves her hand dismissively. "I don't know. It's not like it was a big deal. We were out late one night, and we got caught."

"Wait, are you saying there's a curfew?"

"No, it wasn't that." She looks down, almost like she's embarrassed to admit her next words. "We were out past the city limits. We were looking for the Broken City."

I sit very still. Her words send tingles up my back and excitement fluttering though my heart.

Guards will probably bust through the door any minute now. I glance toward the hallway and hurriedly ask my next question. "What's the Broken City?"

Someone knocks at the door and I groan.

Kassy frowns. "I'm sorry. Were you expecting someone? You should have just said so, really."

I shake my head and move toward the door. Guard Nev stands on the other side, frowning and glaring around me. "Is someone here with you? I just got a message to break up the party."

Kassy moves to my side and glances at Guard Nev. "Oh, hi."

"You should probably go home, Miss."

Her face fills with fear and she glances at me. "I'm sorry, Hana. I didn't mean to get you in trouble."

"No, it's OK. I promise."

She hurries out the door and rushes down the hall to her own door, glancing at us the whole way.

Guard Nev turns back to me, frowning. "What was that about?"

I want to know more about the place Kassy mentioned, but after Guard Nev's earlier lecture, I'm sure he won't help me. "It was nothing. She was lonely and wanted to talk. She said a few things about the city that I guess she shouldn't have said."

But the fact that she is unhappy here is huge. Are there others who feel the same way she does? Professor Higgins comes to mind.

"Keep to yourself for the rest of the night, will you?"

I have some thinking to do, and I can't do it with Guard Nev around. I nod and close the door.

Sindy arrives at exactly ten o'clock the next morning. It's eerie how punctual she and Supreme Moon are. "I trust you haven't eaten? We will be enjoying brunch with Supreme Moon."

I force a smile and follow her to the elevator. "It seems odd that Supreme Moon has so much time to spend with me."

"He wants to hear about your progress with Professor Higgins. Your work with the Lessers is of much interest to him."

Her words put me on edge. They remind me of when Supreme Moon said he had invested in me. Why does he care so much about what I want to do with the Lessers? He hasn't seemed too concerned with helping them in the past.

The mansion is even more brilliant today than it was two weeks ago. A rainbow of flowers spread across the flower beds, and vines and flowers work their way up the pillars.

"Beautiful, isn't it?" Sindy says. "The gardener planted them just this week."

Beautiful is an understatement. In Middle City 3, there were only small flower beds around the most important buildings. I've only seen flowers like that once before. We had taken a family trip when I was a child, and there was a field of wild flowers during a hike.

Supreme Moon awaits us in the dining room. He stands when we enter and waves for us to have a seat. "Professor Higgins tells me your classes are going well."

"Yes." I smile, going for innocent, but it's hard when I'm not sure how to take Professor Higgins' reaction to my statement about God.

"Please tell me about it. He says you had a breakthrough idea about training them."

I shift in my seat as a servant puts eggs on my plate. "I thought we could have the more self-disciplined Lessers—the ones who run the businesses or lead the others—teach their fellow Lessers. They can train them to garden, to run a business, or to use basic math skills. If they were more self-sufficient, they would depend less on the society as a whole."

Supreme Moon pulls back. "Brilliant. With all my advisors, I can't believe no one has ever suggested such a thing."

I hate it—I loathe it—but his words make me sit a little taller. For the first time ever, I see how it was that he became the Great Supreme. He makes you feel like a genius.

The rest of the meal passes uneventfully, and we discuss more of what I've learned in class. By the end of it, I'm even comfortable enough to mention I feel held back by the other students.

"I hope your passion will wear off on them," Supreme Moon assures me quickly. "You don't mind, I hope."

"It's fine," I say.

He walks Sindy and me to the front door, and as he opens it, Guard Nev and the secretary from Supreme Moon's office walk up the steps. They freeze when they see us, but it's pretty obvious they were enjoying one another's company.

"Guard Nev," Supreme Moon says icily. "You may escort Hana home."

Guard Nev's skin turns as red as the flowers in the newly planted flower garden. "Yes, sir," he says, snapping to attention.

Supreme Moon turns to the secretary. His face isn't necessarily venomous, but I wouldn't call it pleasant. "Fallon, you may come inside."

She pushes past me, not meeting anyone's eye, and I step outside before I get caught in the door that Sindy is quickly closing.

Guard Nev and I stand on the steps for a moment. He shifts back and forth, almost like he's considering barging into the Mansion. Finally, he turns to lead the way to a transporter.

The drive home is quiet, but I am reminded of Supreme Moon's person, and I'm ashamed that for the last two hours, I have allowed him to fool me.

We reach my apartment without ever speaking a single word. Guard Nev doesn't even watch as I head to the stairs. An idea forms in my mind, but I'm not sure how to pull it off. I glance one last time at Guard Nev's indifferent frame. If ever I wanted to sneak away, now is the time.

I eat quickly, barely taking time to taste the food. If I want to make a break for it, now would be the best time. Guard Nev is newly distracted. He won't notice me sneaking out the back door. I take my time going down the steps. If he's watching me, then I need to look casual. At the bottom of the stairs, I pause and hold my breath. Will he come?

One Mississippi, two Mississippi, three Mississippi. He doesn't come, so I push through the back door and into the alley. My steps are quick now, and I make it to the corner and peek around. No guard in sight. He really didn't see me, and I'm really free to do some exploring. The possibilities are endless.

I make my way toward the Training Dome for one reason—if Guard Nev were to realize I was missing then he would look at the Lake first.

A transporter zips past and I watch it go. Taking one would get me to the dome faster, but still I hesitate. Few things allow me to feel at home, but walking is one of them. I keep walking.

The Training Dome sparkles in the sun as it

always does. A guard sits at the gate. He looks as bored as ever. "Name?"

"Hana Norfolk."

He glances at his HELP comp and his bored look changes to a frown.

Uh oh.

"Miss Norfolk, I'm going to have to ask you to stay here for a minute."

Great.

My first instinct is to run like I did the first time I ever sneaked out at home. I was caught by a guard while trying to meet up with Fischer's group of Christians. That didn't end so well, so in spite of my instincts, I make myself to stay put.

Only a few minutes pass when a transporter arrives. Guard Nev climbs out, his nostrils flared and his eyes shooting flames of fury at me.

"Identify," the gate-guard says.

Guard Nev holds out his arm and the other guard runs his HELP comp over it. It makes a beeping sound and the guard nods. "Nice time, Guard."

Guard Nev doesn't reply. He jerks his thumb toward the transporter. "Get in." His words are as chilly as the Mississippi in the winter.

I climb in, frustration and shame running through me.

"I thought you were better than that," he says. It's so unlike him to open up this way that I stare at him. "You took advantage of me."

It hits me then that he thinks we're friends. He's opened up to me and I've opened up to him. He knows my mother. He was beginning to think he could trust me. I let him down.

I sink into the seat of the transporter, wishing I

could disappear. "I'm sorry."

He doesn't reply and we make the rest of the ride in silence. At my building he walks me all the way up to my apartment, and when I move to enter, he positions himself to the right of the door, his hands clasped in front of him. He's keeping watch directly outside my door.

Perfect. The one true friend I might have made in Greater City, and I just ruined it. He's never going to help me now.

17

Guard Nev remains silent as he walks me to class the next morning. Supreme Moon humiliated him, but what's worse is I humiliated him. He is angry.

We ride the vac chamber to the third floor, and Professor Higgins waits for me in the hallway.

"Hana, may I speak with you in private?" He glances at Guard Nev, but Guard Nev doesn't move. He frowns at the professor instead.

"Of course," I say, surprised at Guard Nev's rude behavior. I step away from him. Thankfully, he doesn't follow.

"We will be taking a trip to Lesser City 1 this week. I know you are searching for someone—that's been obvious. That isn't allowed. Are you aware?"

Why is he telling me this? I shift uncomfortably. "I'm aware."

He presses something into my hand. "Use this. No one will question you." He smiles and hurries away.

A glance at Guard Nev shows that he's watching me. I don't dare look at what Professor Higgins gave me until I'm alone, whenever that is. Squeezing the item in my palm, I rejoin Guard Nev and we walk to class. "He said we'll be taking our first tour of a Lesser City. Will you be coming with us?"

"I don't know," he says. His words are clipped.

"Have you ever been to one?" I watch his face, gauging his reaction. The last time we spoke of Lessers, he said I would send them to their deaths.

"A few," he says. His face is neutral enough, but his hands clench and unclench constantly.

Was Guard Nev a Lesser? I never would have thought such a thing, except it happened with Fischer. And me, of course. We'd both been promoted instead of demoted. Maybe it happened to Guard Nev, too.

Class begins and Professor Higgins announces our trip for tomorrow. Most of the kids grumble, making it clear they want nothing to do with the Lessers.

Berry holds up a hand. "Wait everyone. You never know, we might make a difference. Wouldn't having a more productive, more powerful nation benefit us all?"

Several of the trainees raise their eyebrows, including me. Has he lost his mind? Last week he was willing to throw me to the Lessers, permanently.

"You've had a change of opinion," Professor Higgins says. "Care to expound?"

"I spoke with my father on the subject. He says I can be a pioneer. I can lead the way to Lesser reform." He says this while looking at me. I'm not sure what he's getting at, but the chill in his stare makes me turn away.

"Well, I applaud you," Professor Higgins says. "I wish that more of you would follow Berry's example."

Berry keeps his eyes on Professor Higgins now, but I can't take my eyes off the back of his head. Something strange is going on with him.

"He's full of it," Kassy says. She sits beside me like she usually dose, but she leans close. "I hope I didn't get you in trouble with the big guy." Her gaze moves to the door where Guard Nev sits.

She's never asked why I always have a guard with me. I'm thankful for that.

"No, it was fine," I whisper.

She watches him for another second, then turns back to me. "Good. I don't want to get you in any extra trouble."

I turn to her but she's already looking at the professor. I stare for a moment before turning away. Maybe she knows more than I give her credit for.

Professor Higgins moves on to discuss economics. He says that people must provide enough for themselves, but when they also provide enough to trade, they make a profit. They can gain wealth and power when this happens.

Our country is poor, he says, except for the Greaters. According to our teachings, we barely have enough to feed ourselves.

Maybe I could believe that Supreme Moon truly is trying to better the country. That he is trying to help the Lessers as well as train up leaders who can forge us on to bigger crops and industries, allowing for trade.

Maybe I could believe that, if I didn't know there are other Lesser cities that are producing far more than we can consume, right now.

Confusion muddles my thinking. Supreme Moon is a terrible person. Haven't I seen it for myself? He demoted Mom because she was sick, and he brought me here for his own gain. My apartment is monitored every moment of every day.

He isn't good, no matter what these discussions would lead me to believe. But it looks like he has almost everyone else fooled.

Training finally ends and we leave for the day. Guard Nev follows behind me, not speaking. I'm thankful he isn't in the mood to lecture me. I want to get home and into my bathroom so I can examine whatever it was that Professor Higgins gave me before class.

I jog up the second, fourth, sixth floors. Finally, I reach my landing. I rush to my apartment and practically run to the bathroom. Once the door is firmly in place, I pull the pouch from my pocket and empty the contents into my hand.

A small vial of—blood? Wrapped around the vial is a note. I read it carefully, but only one word is printed in Professor Higgins' neat handwriting. *Scanner*.

I don't understand what he's telling me. The only scanners I know are the thumb scanners to open certain doors, like the elevator and Records.

The blood swirls as I turn the vial over. Maybe the scanners don't scan thumbprints at all. Everything in Greater City is different, unexpected. Maybe the scanners are checking something else entirely.

DNA? It must be what opens Records.

My throat swells with tears and my eyes burn. He has given me a way to open Records and find Mom. I don't know why he would suddenly decide to do this, not when he seemed so appalled that I knew someone in a Lesser file, but I'm thankful.

I tuck the vial into my pocket, and will keep it with me always so I can get inside Records the first chance that comes along. After I wash my face and change clothes, I settle in to eat supper.

Tomorrow is our first trip to Lesser City 1. Will I find Mom there? I won't know unless I can get into that room, but I won't be able to do that without getting away from Guard Nev. Someone is always there, waiting and watching, ready to stop me. I toy with the idea of sneaking out again—if I got caught, Guard Nev would never trust me again. He'd probably take me to Supreme Moon himself.

On the other hand, it may be my only way to find Mom.

The decision is no decision at all. I have to go.

The only way to get out is waiting for Guard Nev to leave. He can't sleep in the lobby. He's dressed in fresh clothes each morning, which means he leaves at some point and returns. This is my window of opportunity to get out of this building.

Whatever happens, I cannot get caught again.

I sit at the window in my apartment, pretending to watch my comp. A movie plays that looks like it might be funny, but I don't care. All I can focus on is the street that runs seven stories below.

I pass the time by writing another letter to Keegan. This time I don't stop myself from admitting that I miss him like crazy, but I still don't write the words I would have given away so easily before—I love you. How can I say it if there's no future for us? Religion isn't the only reason we aren't together. Now social status also keeps us apart. I didn't know it before, and I'm sure Keegan doesn't know, but I do know it now. I tuck the letter inside my pocket for the morning, ready to mail it first thing tomorrow.

Hours tick by. My eyes grow heavy and I glance at the clock, but I have to haul myself up to remove the pillow. It reads eleven o'clock. I yawn and turn back to the window. A guard walks down the street and stops at my building. I frown.

A replacement. Why hadn't I considered this?

Stupid of me.

How am I going to get past a replacement?

A few minutes later, Guard Nev emerges and

heads south toward the Training Dome. I've heard the military bases are in that direction, but I've never seen them. I haven't seen most parts of the city, which I don't like. Learning the city would give me the most opportunity to find the answers I'm looking for.

But that will come later, when I have time for other things. Tonight I only have time for one.

After Guard Nev disappears from view, I know it's time to figure out a plan of action. I've never met the new guard, and he has no reason to believe I will try to leave during his watch. He's never seen me, and he's definitely never caught me trying to escape. Catching him off guard should be simple. I hope.

18

I drift off sometime after one o'clock, but my eyes snap open as soon as the sun peeks through my window. The glass immediately changes to clear and my apartment lights up. I toss a pillow over the clock, hoping the guard downstairs isn't paying attention, and I dash around my apartment, pulling on pants and shoes, and brushing my hair.

My meals for the day haven't arrived yet, and my stomach growls. Can I make it through the day without something for breakfast?

I don't have time to think about food. I grab the first thing I come to in the cabinet, which happens to be bread and I stuff it in my mouth as I scoot through the hallway. It's my goal to not be seen by the cam disks, but their angle makes it impossible to go unnoticed.

Please don't let the guard be watching.

I reach the stairs and push the tree from in front of the door, and I bolt down the steps. I have to stop once when I get choked on my bread. Too bad I didn't think to bring along some water. When I finally reach the bottom, I stop. What will I say if he's there, waiting?

Taking one last breath, I push through the door.

The alley behind the building is empty. A transporter zips by on the street, but there is no other noise, no other citizens out this early.

One Mississippi, two Mississippi, three Mississippi. I count the old rhyme from Middle City 3.

Being on the Mississippi River front, it had been a game.

When no guard comes rushing around the corner to catch me, I hurry to the street. No walking for me, it might take me too long. I walk a block north and then raise my hand for a transporter. The shiny machine stops in front of me, and I climb in. "The Training Dome."

The transporter moves soundlessly through the streets. By this time in Middle City 3, the city would be teaming with people, but in Greater City, the streets are deserted. I make it there in record time and climb out to hurry to the guard station.

Just as I'd hoped, the guard barely glances at me. "I'm here to report for training."

"Name?"

"Hana Norfolk." I beg my heart to beat calmly.

He pushes the button and returns to his seat. "Go ahead."

The gate swings open and I sigh in relief, then hurry onto campus. My feet pound out my heart's staccato as I race for the door. I stop and take a deep breath before the door slides open and I step inside. Be calm. Act naturally.

No one is in the lobby, but the HELP comp glows a bright blue. I step into the vac chamber and steel myself for the whooshing that will take me to the second floor in the blink of an eye. I've gotten better at arranging myself correctly, and now the air barely blows a hair out of place.

A woman on the second floor passes me and smiles. I hem-haw around until she's out of sight, then I bolt to Records. Looking around, I'm always aware someone might be watching me. A guard or even the oddly lifelike HELP comp. I have to appear to belong here.

I grip the vial of blood in my fist as I approach the DNA scanner, and, when I'm close, I pull out the tiny cork and pour the blood on my fingertip. The scanner flashes constantly, as it always does.

Lord, let this work. You know how I want to find Mom.

I press my finger onto the scanner and the laser reads the DNA of Professor Higgins' blood.

Clear flashes across the screen, and the door slides open.

I use the inside of my shirt to wipe off the blood, and I hurry inside.

Shelves line the massive room from floor to ceiling.

Rows and rows of shelves.

How will I ever find anything in here? Professor Higgins has never taken an excessive amount of time, so there must be a system. I move through the aisles, looking for some form of help. *Help!*

To my right is a small HELP comp. I tap it and it whirs to life. A search bar blinks on screen, and I have to think fast. Searching for Mom's name might raise a red flag. Maybe I can search medical transfers.

I tap in the words and wait the millisecond before results pop up. A list of names fills the screen.

My breath catches.

Most of them are Middles transferred to Lesser hospitals. Relief washes over me like warm rain. I didn't cause Mom's demotion—it is common practice.

It's only been a few weeks, so finding Mom's name doesn't take long. Instead of tapping it, I look at the reference number. Aisle fourteen. Each aisle is marked overhead, and I jog through the maze to the right row, then pull out the box and search for her file.

"Come on, come on!" I say. Where is it? Someone could walk in any minute, and they might know I'm not supposed to be here.

I dig through the entire box, but the file isn't there. I sigh and lean my head against the wall. This can't be happening. Why would someone else have her file? I replace the box and close down HELP, then move to the door and wave my hand over the sensor to get out.

The hallways are still mostly empty as I make my way to the vac chamber. Up or down? I might be able to make it home before Guard Nev arrives. Even if I can't, I doubt he'll turn me in, but it's better for him to see me than to wait and then report me missing—again.

I zip down to the first floor and wave down a transporter. It takes me to a mailing station first, and I drop Keegan's letter into the box then hurry home.

Guard Nev paces the sidewalk in front of the building as I approach. I climb out and Guard Nev stares at me, his hands behind his back. "Where have you been?" his words aren't spoken kindly or even in a neutral tone. He is furious.

"I was at the Training Dome," I admit.

"How did you get out?"

"I snuck out. The other guard isn't as observant as you."

"Why?"

I sigh and turn toward the Training Dome. "Can we talk about it on the way?"

He huffs and begins walking, zooming right by me. I hurry to catch up. "I wanted to look at some things, and I knew you wouldn't let me."

"In Records?" His voice is sarcastic; like he's

pointing out that he knows what I do.

I stop and tug on his uniform. He frowns and stops along with me. "My mom was demoted due to an illness. I just want to know where they took her." I'm hoping this will resonate with him. He did know her, after all.

His eyes narrow. "You're traveling today."

I was hoping he wouldn't put that together. "Yes."

"You cannot look for her. It's illegal."

My heart picks up speed, but I don't speak. He wouldn't stop me, would he?

I like Guard Nev, and I hope that someday we really can be friends, but I don't care what he tries today. I will do whatever it takes to find her.

"Let's go," he finally says.

I hurry to catch up, but I can't keep the bounce from my step. Today I might get to see Mom.

19

The training dome is full when we arrive—when I re-arrive. Trainees chatter in the classroom, and their excitement fills the air in spite of their earlier moans of protest over visiting a Lesser City. I slip into my usual seat near the front of the class. No one speaks to me, and I speak to no one, but Kassy bumps her shoulder against mine and smiles.

I look around and consider the other kids in the room. What will happen to these students in the future? Fischer and his people wanted to change the country, spread deliverance in Christ. What will become of those in Greater City who refuse to believe?

The goal I set off to accomplish seems almost nonexistent now that I'm actually here. How can I spread Christ's message when I'm alone? When I can barely leave my apartment?

Professor Higgins steps to the front of the class and I'm reminded that I may not be alone. Maybe there are others.

I tune out my memories and focus on the professor. He sent me to Records to find something, or someone, but Mom wasn't to be found. Should I tell him that the HELP comp showed her name, but her file was missing?

Now is not the time, so I listen to his boring instructions on keeping our mouths shut in front of the Lessers. The biggest concern is not letting them know all of the extras the Greaters receive. He instructs us to smile at them, interact with them, but mostly to watch them. We are to glean information and bring it back to this room for dissection and planning.

We file out the back of the building—which I've never seen—and into a long vehicle. It's solid black, and almost iridescent. Once we're seated and strapped in, the machine whirs to life and we begin driving.

"Why do we have to take this ancient transporter?" one of the trainees asks. I had wondered the same thing.

"The Lessers don't have transporters," Professor Higgins explains. "They aren't aware of the technology available to the Greaters. It's important we keep it that way. So we're taking the bus."

"What else don't they have?" someone else asks.

I frown. Don't these Greaters learn anything in school?

"They don't have HELP comps, or even old computers. They don't have Tech Meds or food deliveries each day."

He goes on, but my mind is focused on one word. Medicine. I am Greater. I have access to chemotherapy, along with a long list of other medications—Tech Meds.

The knowledge sets my heart to racing. If I can find Mom, if I can get my hands on chemo, then I can try to save her.

I glance back at Guard Nev who sits in the last seat of the vehicle. He watches the city pass us by. I turn to my own window, calculating a plan. All I have to do is find the hospital. Finding her might be easier than I had hoped, but will he try to stop me?

The plan comes together in my mind and I smile.

Kassy sits with me and she chatters on and on about the latest movie she saw. I smile and nod as I need to, but my mind is on one thing only.

The drive takes an hour or so. The bus lurches to a stop in front of a gate, and two guards approach. They speak with the bus driver, and the gates swing open a few minutes later. We pull through and I crane my neck for a better look. This is Lesser City 1.

I wonder what I'll see here—will it be like I've always been taught, or was Fischer telling the truth? I have a feeling that Fischer was right, and the people I will find here are just like me.

My eyes slip closed and I think about Fischer. It's not something I've done very often since coming to Greater City. I can almost feel his hand on my face. It feels like a hundred years ago.

The drive into the old city isn't disappointing or surprising. It looks similar to Middle City 3, only more crowded and a bit more shambled. The people look worn and dirty, but not unhappy. I search their faces for the vacant look Ava wore after taking the pills, but no one here appears that way.

People watch us drive past with unmasked curiosity. They probably never see cars on the road, since they don't get gasoline allowances. Their clothes hang on their bodies like bags, their bones visible beneath their skin. Most of their cheeks are sunken into their faces.

My heart lurches and I think of Jamie. Is this how she is forced to live?

The vehicle parks and we file out. Most of the students press together, unwilling to interact at all. My nerves are on high alert, but I force myself to do better. I step forward and wave at a child in the street. "Hi there. What's your name?"

"Micah." His voice is soft and sweet, but his eyes are empty and unhealthy looking.

"It's nice to meet you Micah. I'm Hana."

He smiles shyly and hurries away. I watch him stop at a woman and point at us. She must be his mother. I wave and smile, but she frowns and hurries away.

How can I blame her? I am one of them. I am to be feared.

The realization makes me sad. I am here to help these people, but it will take a lot to get them to trust me.

Gray is all around us. Gray streets, dusty gray buildings, and even a gray sky. The Lessers' clothes are all dull shades of black or gray or brown.

Another thing I notice immediately is the quiet. The lack of noise is unnerving. The people move through the streets in quiet determination. Their clothes don't swish, their breaths are light, and no one chatters among themselves like the trainees had done this morning at the Training Dome.

"Where are the people who qualify to teach?" I ask Professor Higgins. My voice carries in the still air. "Where are the people who could train the others?"

His brow wrinkles as he thinks. "Lesser 1 is poor. There are very few shop owners. Not all of the Lesser cities are this bad, but this one has little hope of producing profitable citizens."

"But there are a few, right? Where can we find them?"

He pulls a small HELP comp from his shirt pocket and scrolls through the information. "The commerce district is in the center of the city. That is where we'll find the shop owners and other workers."

A thought strikes me then. "If the Lessers Test as Lesser, what occupational assignments are they given?"

"It depends," Professor Higgins says as we walk. "Those who are deemed fit are sent to clean the streets or buildings in Middle cities. Others are assigned work in the hospital here, or the child care centers, or shops."

While their own city wastes away, the Lessers keep Middle cities clean. The thought saddens me. "What about the people who don't work?"

He shrugs. "They probably never tested."

I look into the faces of the people we pass, and an ache fills me. What could they be, if given the chance?

Something he said sticks out to me, though, and it's exactly what I was hoping for. I latch onto it. "What kind of medical care are the Lessers given?"

I'm suddenly aware of Guard Nev beside me, scowling at me.

I ignore him as any Greater would.

"Their hospitals aren't much. We can tour this city's, if you wish."

Some of the other trainees moan, but Berry steps forward. "I think that is a fine idea. We need to get a clear picture of those who can't help society. Unhealthy citizens aren't profitable, wouldn't you agree, Middle?"

His gaze is unnerving, but I shake it off. "I suppose." His calling me by my former ranking is annoying, but it's not what bothers me most. He seems to be implying something else altogether, and he wants me to get it.

The Lessers part like the Red Sea for Moses—I read that story last night—as we walk through the dirty streets. Trash piled on the corners stinks of refuse and is infested with maggots. Some of the trainees gag and turn away. It's hard, but I manage to keep my face forward.

After a few blocks, we reach a single story building. *Medical Clinic* is painted on the front in crude, mismatched letters. "If you would like to see the inside, follow me," Professor Higgins says. Only a handful of us go in, including Guard Nev. The entire hospital is housed in one single room. Beds line the walls with only a few feet separating each one. The air is stifling and stale, and the only light coming in is from the windows. How could anyone get well here?

I scan the beds quickly, but no one resembling Mom is in this large room. It's almost a relief. As Professor Higgins speaks, I seek out a medic. One stands at a sink, washing supplies. She smiles as I approach.

"Excuse me, can you tell me if you've had a patient named Mya Norfolk?" I say the name slowly, as if that will help her recognize it. Each millisecond of waiting is agony. She may have been moved, or maybe she never came. There are other options, but I don't want to consider them.

But the medic shakes her head. "I'm sorry. I've never heard that name."

"That's OK. Thanks anyway."

Guard Nev resumes his place beside me. "It's useless to try. There is no hope."

"There is always hope," I bite out.

He stares at me curiously, but I don't explain. Let him think what he wants.

The rest of the trip has lost its appeal. I'm ready to cross this city off the list and move on to the next one. I come very close to asking Professor Higgins when we travel again, but I don't want to seem too obvious. Besides, how many times can I get away with asking to see the hospital?

We return to Greater City after a couple of hours, and everyone seems happy to be back. I'm ashamed when I realize that I'm happy to be back, too.

Guard Nev walks me back to my apartment. "Don't even think about sneaking out tonight."

"I won't. I didn't find what I was looking for, anyway."

His eyes narrow and I can almost feel his curiosity. He doesn't ask questions, though. He almost never does.

"Good night, Guard Nev. I'll see you in the morning." I push through the door to the stairs and jog up the steps. Mom isn't in Lesser City 1. At least it is something. It's better than no information at all. Now I can focus my search on Lesser 2. Until I can get my hands on her file, it will have to do.

20

My HELP comp dings as I get ready for training the next morning. I've set it to notify me any time Keegan is performing at the concert arena, so I hurry to see what the ding means. *Requested Information* blinks on screen and I quickly tap the link. I smile as Keegan's name pops up. He'll be playing tonight, and I will be there.

At training, Professor Higgins surprises me as soon as class starts. "We will be visiting Lesser City 2 on Friday. They are a bit more prosperous than Lesser 1, but not much more so."

Two trips in one week is a good thing, even though it seems odd. Professor Higgins had warned me the focus would shift away from the Lessers, only it hasn't.

I tuck the information away for later as we begin discussion on what we saw in Lesser City 1. Berry points at that if there was more incentive to do well, such as higher allowances, then more Lessers might be motivated to become productive.

"And what if we run out of ways to reward them?" I ask. "What if something happens to our country which disallows us from providing extra? Those who worked only for the reward will stop working, and our society will fall further."

Berry sneers. "Like anything can happen to us."

Is he serious? "It's happened in the past."

He rolls his eyes. "Then what do you suggest?"

"Show them how much better their lives will be. It won't work with everyone, but I believe it will work with most of them. There is a saying they used in the Early Days. Give a man a fish and he'll eat for a day. Teach a man to fish, and he'll eat for a lifetime. It's the same principle."

Some of the trainees giggle and Berry speaks up. "The Early Days? You're way out of touch."

Again I wonder what they teach here. I turn away from him and look to Professor Higgins for guidance. He smiles at me and moves the conversation along. I'm not sure, but I think I see pride in his eyes.

"Don't worry about Berry," Kassy whispers. "No one likes him."

I smile at her, but I can't help worrying about his behavior toward me.

The day moves on and our assignment is to draw up a model that will help the people in Lesser 1, based on what we saw while we were there. Professor Higgins instructs us to pair up. Thank goodness for Kassy, because no one else would consider working with me.

We start with outlining our thoughts on paper, and then Kassy pulls over the small HELP comp each team has available. She begins tapping, using functions that are completely foreign to me. After just a few minutes she has entered all of my ideas and an entire graph pops up on screen.

"How did you do that?"

She grins with pride. "I can teach you a few tricks."

Tricks I can use. "I would love that."

By the end of the day my mind is exhausted.

Professor Higgins pulls me aside when the other students have gone. "You did well today, Hana. Supreme Moon will be happy with your progress. He's quite interested in your ideas and he'll be glad to see your model. It's the best in the class."

I smile, not sure how to respond to this information. Supreme Moon is oddly interested in the Lessers and my ideas. I realize this is why I was brought here in the first place, but I can't be that important.

Thinking about it irks me and I change the subject, instead. "Can I ask you a question, Professor Higgins? Why did you help me yesterday?"

His excited face falls a bit, and he glances around. "I see a little more in you, that's all."

"What do you mean?" If I can get him to say anything about God—anything at all—then I will know for sure there are other Christians in the city. I will be able to find others to help me learn, and who might know how to further spread the message.

He pats my hand and smiles again. "You have passion, Hana. The other trainees here? They don't."

I force a smile and nod. "Thank you, Professor Higgins."

Guard Nev joins me and we make a quick exit. I don't want to linger any longer than I have to because the professor's words confuse me. He seems to sway one direction some days and a different direction on other days.

"I plan to go to a concert tonight," I warn Guard Nev as we walk. "My friend will be there."

He nods.

"You're not going to tell me all the reasons I shouldn't?" I say, teasing.

Maybe he smiles, maybe he doesn't—but he doesn't reply. At least it appears he's forgiven me.

I eat what the food delivery brings me, and then I retreat to the bathroom for a few minutes of not being watched. The warm bath water relaxes the tension from my muscles. How do the Greaters do it? Spending every minute of every day being watched—it's too much for me. I need time to unwind, to just be myself and not worry what the world is thinking.

After bathing, I put on a pair of only slightly fraying brown pants, and a knit top the color of a sunrise. I let my hair air dry while I read a few verses in my Bible, then I jog down to meet Guard Nev. My excitement grows with each step that takes me closer to Keegan. Did he get my last letter? I want to tell him I visited a Lesser City, and that I was able to look for Mom. And I just want to see him.

I find a seat and expect to see Guard Nev loitering at the end of the row like last time, but he's standing in the aisle, looking across the arena at a group of women awaiting the music. His face almost looks happy, which is very unusual for him.

Scanning the group of women, I see why. Supreme Moon's secretary, Fallon, is in the group. She throws back her head and laughs at something one of the others said. Her face radiates happiness, and I can see why Guard Nev is attracted to her—she's beautiful with her long, wavy, blond hair and her perfectly shaped smile.

After a moment of staring, he seems to remember me and glances my way. I grin and shoo him away with my hands. He frowns and shakes his head.

"Go!" I mouth.

He looks at her one last time, then strides that

way, and I turn to the stage to wait for Keegan. Tonight he is the fourth act, and it feels like an eternity has passed before he finds me in the crowd and smiles. From the first note he strums, I am hooked. The song is slow and deep. He sings of a love no evil can penetrate.

When the song finishes, he heads backstage. I look around for Guard Nev, but he's nowhere to be found. Oh well. He'll know where he can find me, if he looks.

Keegan waits for me, smiling. "No tail?"

"I don't know where he went," I say, glancing behind me again. We are alone in the hallway, but that doesn't make me happy anymore. I'm Greater, and I can be alone with Keegan. But he is still Middle, and being alone with me is against the law.

This must be why Guard Nev's being alone with the secretary is a problem.

I glance at Keegan, and I am super aware that I don't want to get him in trouble. I look to the arena one last time, almost hoping for Guard Nev to appear but being relieved when he doesn't.

"Do you need to wait for him?" Keegan asks when I hesitate.

"I don't want to get you in trouble."

He nods toward his prep room. "I'm not worried. Come on in."

I scan the hallway for small, metal disks that might be watching us, and I follow him inside and sit on a couch in the corner. Once he puts his equipment away, he sits beside me. "So? What's new?"

I laugh, almost giddy at being with him. "I went to a Lesser City. It was basically like what we've been told, except the people weren't terrible. They were more scared than anything." I tell him about Professor Higgins helping me look for Mom, but also how

Supreme Moon is interested in my work. "Why do you think he cares so much, when it's been this way for two centuries and no one has cared?"

Keegan frowns and looks at the floor. "I've been hearing things as I've asked around. Most of the guards are from the Middle cities. I hear them talk, and they've mentioned the prison. They say it's a training camp."

"What are they training for?"

He clears his throat and looks back at me. "War."

Chill bumps prick my arms and I rub my hands over them to warm me.

Keegan reaches out. "Let me do that."

I know I should stop him, but I can't make myself do it. His hands are warm and strong, and after a moment I'm not at all cold. It's more like I'm on fire. "Is that better?" he asks.

He's so close that I can smell the soap on his skin. His warm breath tickles my neck, and then he kisses me, right on the lips. He's tentative at first, but then his kiss is more searching.

It's the first time I've ever been kissed—really kissed—and it is amazing. I kiss him back and he pulls away. He swallows hard and turns away from me. "Maybe having the guard around is a good idea."

I laugh, nervous, and nod. "I know."

His gaze finds mine again, and it's questioning. I can almost hear his thoughts. Is it OK that he kissed me? Do I still feel about him like he feels about me?

Yes and yes.

How am I ever supposed to turn him down? He isn't bad. In fact, there's nothing further from the truth. He is infinitely good.

And yet, there is one huge area where we don't

agree, and there is one gaping law keeping us apart. "Have you done any thinking?"

He knows what I mean right away and he shrugs. "Yeah. I ask about that when I ask about the prison."

"And?"

He sighs and stands, then begins pacing the room. "I'm still not sure, Hana. It's too different. Why would Someone in control let things get so out of control?"

His argument makes sense, and I don't know enough to explain otherwise. "All I know is what I feel. I know the change in me is real."

He watches me, his pacing stopped. He nods. "I can get that."

Hope revives in me. For now, it is enough.

The door bursts open and Guard Nev storms in. He glances at me then Keegan, and when he sees we're apart, he calms down a fraction. "You should have waited."

"I didn't see you," I say. "I did look."

He has no rebuttal for that. "I think it's best if we go." He looks around the room the same way I did earlier, probably searching for cam disks.

"Did you get my letter? Will you write me again?"

"Of course," Keegan says.

I wrap my arms around his waist. Who cares if Guard Nev sees that? Keegan's arms are safe.

"Soon," he says.

I nod. "Soon."

21

The drive to Lesser City 2 takes longer than our first trip away from Greater City. Professor Higgins explains it is further away. He says the Lesser cities are numbered by their distance from Greater City.

I crane my neck to catch sight of any building that might be a hospital as we ride through the streets, but nothing pops out at me. I doubt I will be able to talk the group into touring another medical facility. After the last tour, two girls caught some strange virus. Lucky for them Greater City is equipped with Tech Meds.

Excitement makes sitting still pure torture. I want to get off this vehicle and search high and low for Mom. She could be in this city. I tap my foot on the floor of the vehicle. Maybe there's a way I can get separated and make it look like an accident, though getting away from Guard Nev is next to impossible. Where is Supreme Moon's secretary when I need her?

"Don't even think about it," Guard Nev whispers when we step off the bus.

"What?"

"I see you scoping the city."

"Why is it so important to you that I don't do this?" I snap. At first I glance around, hoping no one heard me, but then I remember there are no cam disks here. They wouldn't waste the resources on Lessers.

He pauses at my words, but then he growls in

frustration. "I have been ordered to watch you. I cannot let you do something illegal under my watch."

"You do illegal things yourself," I accuse. "You were alone with that woman. Why do you get to break laws but I don't, when the laws are equally absurd?"

He growls then turns and marches to the back of the group.

Professor Higgins leads us on a tour of the business district here. The people are slightly less disheveled than in Lesser 1. The buildings are slightly better kept, and the people's cheeks aren't quite so hollow. This gives me hope that by the time we get to Lesser 3, or even Lesser 8, the people will be doing very well.

An idea forms in my mind. "Can we transfer people between the Lesser cities for training? That way the more prosperous people of this city could help the people in the other cities." Why didn't I think of this before?

Professor Higgins' eyebrows shoot up and he nods. "Excellent suggestion, Hana."

Berry steps forward like he's going to rebut my idea, but finally he steps back into place. There is no arguing that my idea is a good one.

The rest of the trip passes slowly. Professor Higgins never mentions the city's hospital, and even though I scan the area constantly, I never see one. Disappointment hits me like a snowy wind when we reload onto the bus. If Mom is in Lesser City 2, I will never know.

Kassy comes over when we get home, and she shows me a few new tricks for my HELP comp. I can download any of the programs I saw on the HELP comps on the street right onto my own comp. She also shows me how to block certain security programs, but she does it in a way that the comp won't pick up on it. I thank her and promise to try it out later—and I will, but it's so new that I'm sure I'll mess it up.

Two days later, Professor Higgins springs a third trip on us. We will be going to Lesser City 3 immediately.

My ears perk up at this news. Lesser 3 is Fischer's home town. His mother and father are there. Maybe they've heard from him, even though I haven't.

This brings another thought. Has Fischer purposefully stopped communicating with me?

I push the thought away. He wouldn't do that—not that I have a right to expect him to pursue me, not when I've been much more interested in Keegan these days.

The ride to Lesser City 3 is further still. For the first time I wish, right along with the other students, that we could take one of the newer, smoother-riding transporters instead of the old bus.

As we pass through the city, Professor Higgins takes us to a specific set of shops. "These stores have been deemed especially useful to the city," he explains. "It is here that we will most likely find the more promising Lessers."

He points out a grocer and I'm reminded of Jamie. Maybe one day she'll be able to work in her chosen field, after all.

Fischer's family was prosperous, I remember. The things he described to me line up with what I see. I scan the faces of the people, searching for anyone who resembles the boy with the deep dimples and wavy brown hair, but no one sticks out to me.

Kassy walks beside me as always, scanning faces

but not speaking. She has never given me her thoughts about the Lessers or helping them. What does she think about my passion? I also can't help but wonder what she would think if she knew the truth—that I don't care so much about helping the Lessers these days as I do about finding Mom.

We continue our tour, and the people of Lesser City 3 barely glance at us as they go about their daily business. The shops are small and tidy, and the storefronts are cheerful and bustling. Flowers line some of the sidewalks. The people are clean, and while they're too skinny, their skin isn't the unhealthy gray pallor of the people of Lesser 1 and 2.

The difference between this place and the first two cities is glaring.

"Why is it so different here?" I ask.

Professor Higgins moves to the front of the group to tell us all at once. "These people work harder. They obey the laws and are willing to try new things that the Greaters bring their way. The other cities should aspire to be like the Lessers of City 3."

There is little difference between this city and my own home city of Middle 3. It's almost eerie. What separates one class from another? Worse, what will happen to these people in the future? What if Supreme Moon does as I suggested and forces these people to leave their businesses, homes, and families in order to train the other Lessers? What will happen to this city when the more prosperous leave? Would the end justify the means?

By now the other trainees have stopped griping about whether or not they should have to visit the Lesser cities. Most seem to enjoy seeing new things, now that they've been exposed to it. I think it's good for them. Everyone needs to see the way the Lessers are treated. If they see it, they may come to realize it isn't right. Maybe one of them will come up with a better idea that would keep the people from being forced to leave their homes.

While we walk, I scan the streets for anyone who looks pregnant. I haven't seen many pregnant women in the other cities. Jamie would be several months along by now, but few who we pass have blond hair, and none have large bellies.

We tour a few more blocks when Berry makes his way to me. "It's too bad we won't be visiting another hospital, isn't it?"

I haven't been able to come up with a good reason for finding the hospital, but something in his voice makes me stop. "What makes you think I would want to?"

"Find the hospital? I know it's what you want to see the most. It's too bad we won't be touring it. I have a feeling you would find it beneficial."

He can't know about Mom. How would he?

Still, he must. His words set my heart to racing. "I don't know what you're talking about."

"You know exactly what I'm talking about, and I know exactly what you're searching for. Good luck with that."

I feel like my heart is going to explode right out of my chest. Ba BOOM ba BOOM ba BOOM. Forget Berry. I step around him and push my way to Guard Nev. Kassy frowns after me as I rush away.

"You have to help me," I say, grabbing Guard Nev's arm. "You have to help me find the hospital. She's here. My mom is here." The words tumble out and tears threaten to erupt from my eyes.

"What? I thought you couldn't find her."

"She's here. I know she is. I have to see her. Please, Guard Nev. Help me."

He swallows hard and looks around. "What good is it going to do your mom if you get demoted as well?"

"Supreme Moon won't demote me." I'm surer of these words than I am of anything else right now. He needs me and my ideas. I have no idea why, but I'm sure I'm right.

"And what about me?"

I pause. What about Guard Nev? What about Keegan, for that matter? What if my actions get them demoted?

Memories of Mom's eyes and smile and smell play through my mind. She once told me, "Lessers are the key." It's almost as if she knew this day would come. "Please," I say.

He sighs. "I'll try."

I resist the urge to throw myself at him in a hug. I have a feeling it wouldn't go well on his part.

Berry watches every step I take, but I don't care. Now that I've realized I'm not getting demoted for this, I don't care if Supreme Moon himself were here to stop me.

After a few blocks, Guard Nev takes my elbow. "Follow me. Quickly."

We dart into an alley and the rest of the group moves on without us.

"Keep up with me," he says.

My legs burn as I try to match his long steps. We turn from one alley to another, and then a third before we reach the hospital. This one is larger than the small clinic in Lesser 1. Hope surges through me. Mom might be inside this very building.

I barge inside and straight to the front desk. "I'm looking for a patient. She was brought here a few weeks ago from Middle City 3. Her name is Mya Norfolk."

The woman at the counter frowns. She has no old computer like Fischer had back home. All of her files are stacked in piles behind her and around her. "I'm not sure, sweetie."

"I remember," a different woman says. She steps from behind a pile. "She had the mutation, right?"

I nearly choke with relief, and I nod. They know her. She's here! If I talk, I will cry.

The woman's eyes soften and she pats my hand. "I'm sorry, ma'am. Mya Norfolk had already passed away when she reached the hospital. I remember her, though, because Mya was my mother's name."

"Passed away?" The words come out in a whisper. I'm not even sure it's my own voice.

I try to run, but Guard Nev grabs me. "Just wait," he whispers into my hair. It's then I realize his arms are around me, holding me in place. "Hold on."

I blink several times, my breath coming in short, painful bursts.

"Did you know her well?" the woman asks quietly.

"My mother," I choke out.

The woman takes in my clothes and full cheeks. She frowns. "Why was she here?"

Why was she here? A Lesser when I am obviously more? "Why are any of you here?" I shout. "No one deserves this!"

"Hana!" Guard Nev hisses. Now his grip on me isn't comforting, it's painful. He drags me from the building and into the street.

"You cannot incite some sort of rebellion. Never speak like that again." He shakes me. "Do you understand me?"

Tears burst from my eyes and I sob. Mom is dead. I will never see her again. Was she even given a proper burial? I collapse in his arms and he lets me stay there, sobbing. He says nothing and does nothing. I'm glad because nothing he could say would make this better.

After a few minutes of crying, the woman comes outside. "Miss, I'm sorry. She has a cross, though. Would you like to see it?"

"A cross?"

"Yes ma'am, to remember her by."

I have no idea what she means, but I allow her to lead me through the alley and to the back of the hospital. A field stretches out for miles, and in almost every available space are wooden sticks. They've been nailed together to form a small "t", and it hits me. A cross, like from the Bible.

I've never seen a grave marked with a cross.

"How are you allowed to use a religious symbol?" I ask.

The woman frowns. "What do you mean?"

Her sincerity rips my emotions apart and I look out over the field. Thousands and thousands of crosses cover the land, so much so that almost no grass can be seen.

For two hundred years they have been marking those who died with a cross. Someone, in the very beginning of our country's history, refused to give up their beliefs. They were defying our government even back then, even though the people today aren't aware of the significance. No wonder Fischer and his family found God here. Religion's presence is stronger here than in any of the other cities so far.

"Thank you for showing me," I finally say. "I'm sorry I shouted at you."

She smiles kindly. "It's OK. I understand."

We turn away from the field in silence and walk back to the street.

"Are you OK?" Guard Nev asks.

I take a shaky breath and glance around. "I don't know."

"Are you going to be OK to go back to the group?"

Never. I never want to return to Greater City.

Instead, I nod.

We turn to retrace our steps back to Professor Higgins when someone catches my eye. He's a janitor of sorts, and he empties trash into the garbage bins outside. It's his face that makes me look twice, and I remember how Fischer said his father worked at the hospital. It's what got Fischer interested in being a medic in the first place. This janitor has the same full cheeks and dark, curly hair as Fischer. Could this be Fischer's father?

I quickly approach him. "Excuse me, sir, do you have a son?"

The man pauses and takes in my clothes. I must seem so odd to these people. "Yes, ma'am," he says slowly.

"Is his name Fischer?"

He frowns and shakes his head, but then he pauses. "You must be thinking of Rico's son."

My breath catches and I step forward. "Rico?"

"He's inside. I think he had a son named Fischer. Would you like me to get him for you?"

I glance at Guard Nev who frowns. "Please

hurry," I say. Bossing him around feels wrong on so many levels, but he does as I ask, and a few moments later he reappears with the man named Rico.

"You asked about my son?" Rico asks. He wrings his hands and watches me intently.

"Do you have a grown son named Fischer? One who tested as a Middle?"

To my surprise, tears fill the man's eyes. "Do you have word from him? He wrote faithfully his whole time away, but the letters stopped a few weeks ago."

Hot dread seeps through me at his words. "I haven't spoken to him in a few weeks, either," I admit. "I don't know what happened to him."

Rico's shoulders sag and he drops his head. "Then why have you come?"

I swallow back my fear that Supreme Moon had Fischer killed. It is more likely that he demoted him to a different city — maybe Lesser 4. "I don't know why I approached you, except I remembered Fischer said you worked here. We — we were friends."

The man looks up and watches me curiously. Finally, he nods. "If you hear from him, can you let me know somehow?" He seems to realize what he just asked, or maybe of whom he asked it. "I'm sorry, Miss. I didn't mean disrespect."

I shake my head. "It wasn't disrespect, and I promise to let you know. It was good to meet you."

He nods and I hurry away.

Guard Nev doesn't ask questions. He seems to have accepted that I have a lot of secrets. He obviously has his own.

He takes me back to the rest of the group. Professor Higgins flocks to me, his gray hair askew and his eyes wide with worry. "Where have you been?

I nearly called in the guards." He looks Guard Nev up and down. "The only reason I didn't was because of him."

The absurdity of Professor Higgins' face strikes me as funny in the oddest way. "I'm sorry, Professor. I got lost. Guard Nev found me and helped me back."

"Well, I'm glad you're OK." He continues to watch my face, and I'm sure the evidence of tears is still strong. He doesn't ask though, and soon the tour is over.

We load up and begin the long ride back to Greater City. I can feel Berry's gaze on me, but I don't look at him. Not yet, anyway. I will deal with him later.

I place my hand on the window as we pass through the city gates, and I whisper one last goodbye to Mom.

22

I lie in bed, staring at the ceiling. The auto shutters opened long ago, but I never went to sleep, and the sunlight means nothing to me.

Mom is dead. She's been gone for weeks and we never knew it. Does Dad know? Supreme Moon? If the Great Supreme knows, does he even care?

I have one consolation—she believed in God before she died. I hope—I must believe—that I will see her again in Heaven.

At some point the HELP comp chimes, so I crawl from bed and make my way to it. *Brunch today. Guard Nev will escort you. S.*

They won't let me have a single day off. It must be a strategy, on their part. If they keep me busy, then I won't be able to get into any trouble on my own.

It takes an hour to make me feel human again, and then I make my way down to meet Guard Nev. He greets me at the bottom of the stairs. He's not his usual, distant self today. He almost treats me like an egg that might crack. I don't know if I like it or hate it, so I don't think about it.

The transporter takes us across the city to the Mansion.

"Good morning," Sindy says with a smile. "Supreme Moon is waiting for us in the dining room."

I consider returning the smile, but I just don't have it in me. We walk to the dining room in silence, Guard

Nev trailing behind.

Supreme Moon sits at the table like a king—except he's not. He had no right to sentence Mom to death.

I breathe deeply through my nose so I don't say anything stupid, that he's a fraud, for instance, and I take a seat. Guard Nev moves to stand guard at the door, but Supreme Moon holds out a hand to stop him. "Please, stay. Eat with us."

This is obviously out of Guard Nev's comfort zone because he pauses before he moves to sit beside me.

"Wonderful!" Supreme Moon says. "Now that we're all together, we can begin." He claps his hands and servants bring the platters of food.

Heaping piles of food are loaded onto my plate. More food than I could ever eat. The same for Guard Nev.

Supreme Moon begins to eat, and we follow suit. "I hear you have taken a few excursions into the Lesser cities," he says between bites of egg and potato casserole. Cheese strings from his chin and a servant moves in to wipe it away.

"Yes," I say. "Cities one, two, and three."

His face lights up and he smiles. "Excellent! And how did you find it?"

I shift in my seat. How am I supposed to answer that? I can't pretend that I care about his programs at this particular moment. "They were much like I expected, except the people were better than I was always told."

"That's a unique perception. Professor Higgins tells me you have some promising theories for training the Lessers. How do you propose we implement them immediately?"

"I don't know, sir. I'm only in training." Again the

eerie feeling that he's putting too much trust in me creeps up.

"No one cares about them like you do, Hana." He leans toward me, his words clipped and demanding. "You can help them become more disciplined, more able to follow orders, and ultimately more profitable to us as a country."

Why does he need the Lessers now when he hasn't needed them for all the years of his supremacy? Unless the rumors are correct.

But speaking against him is not an option, especially when his eyes bore into me.

"We would need to test those Lessers who have shown the most promise as teachers—the ones who run shops or grow large crops. Once they're tested and trained, we develop classes and put them at the head to teach the others."

Supreme Moon listens intently, nodding. "And you think they'll cooperate?"

I pause. "Not everyone, no. Some will have to leave their families or businesses, and that will be difficult. The others might not like it either, especially when it comes to training the undisciplined citizens. They'll resist becoming disciplined."

"And how should we deal with that?" He leans toward me, ever eager.

"You could offer incentive—a better place for their family, a place where they can grow gardens so they will have more to eat. Offer them seeds. Winter coats. Perhaps even gasoline. But you would need to be careful with this program, so they don't feel that you owe them more."

As soon as the words leave my mouth my stomach rolls. Did I really just say that? I watch Supreme Moon to see if he realizes what my words mean—I sound exactly like him. I'm helping him do something detestable. Why did I have this idea in the first place?

"Amazing," he says. He sits back and glances at our plates. "Eat, please. I've kept you talking far too long."

Guard Nev continues eating in silence, but I've had my fill.

"Aren't you hungry?" Supreme Moon asks. "It seems you wouldn't want to offend your Great Supreme."

I force a smile and take a small bite. He continues watching, so I take another and another. Finally, I push the plate away. "I'm full now, thank you."

His face changes from excited and kind to chilling. "You will eat more." It isn't a question, and it isn't debatable.

I take another bite and he smiles again. "See? It's not so bad. I figured you would want more, because it seems that you always want more. More freedom than the other citizens, more knowledge than the leaders of the country, more time with a dead mother."

I gasp. My first thought is to lunge at him, and I would do it except Guard Nev grabs me and keeps me in place. "You monster!" I hiss.

"I watched you on the cams. You tried to find her in Records. Didn't though, did you? I wonder why." His last sentence is spoken with an absent stare over my shoulder. He is sincere. He doesn't know where Mom's file is, but I think I do.

"You managed to find her, though, with his help." He nods at Guard Nev. "Did you get to say your goodbyes? She was a good woman. I'm sure she will be prominent in her next life."

My fingers clench so tightly that the nails slice into my skin.

Now he turns to Guard Nev. "She's not the only one who wants more. I hear you visited the concert arena recently."

Guard Nev stiffens and slowly lets me out of his death hold.

"My secretary was there. Or should I say, my former secretary? Yes, sadly I had to release her from her duties. It isn't proper and fitting to have a Lesser as my own, personal secretary."

It takes a second for his words to sink in, but when they do, Guard Nev lunges. There is no one to stop him at first, but other guards rush in and haul him off the Great Supreme's table.

Supreme Moon laughs in delight. "You must have known you were on dangerous ground, Nev. It was foolish of you, really. Perhaps you will be more careful in the future?" He turns back to me. "And you may want to keep this scenario in mind in the future, in regard to your pow-wows with your former neighbor boy. Keegan, isn't it?"

It is a clear warning, and dully noted, but my heart rips in two. Not see Keegan again? He's my only link to home and happiness.

Guard Nev is dragged from the room. I watch him go, wondering if I'll ever see him again, either.

Seconds tick by. When the clamor caused by Guard Nev dies down, I force myself to turn back to Supreme Moon.

"Don't worry about him. He is loyal. He only needed to be reminded of it. I am, however, concerned about you." His voice turns icy and his eyes narrow. "You were searching for your mother. I can understand that. It is done, now, though, and I want your word that you will not continue this nonsense."

I'm hyper aware of everything going on in the room. A servant wiping the counter top. Sindy picking at a fingernail. Supreme Moon watching me.

I clear my throat. "I understand."

"That's not what I want to know. I have no doubt that you 'understand'. I want to make sure you are going to comply."

He isn't giving me specific situations. I do not want to lie, but I have no intention of letting all the corruption go unnoticed.

"I will comply," I finally say. *Please forgive me.*

He smiles and leans back in his chair. "Excellent. Sindy will escort you home."

23

I place the letter in the mail box on my way to the Training Dome in the morning. Surely Keegan won't get in trouble for one last letter. If someone confiscates it they will only find two words. *I'm sorry.*

My mind lingers on Guard Nev. Is he badly hurt? Locked up? Sent away? Supreme Moon said not to worry about him, but I can't trust anything Supreme Moon says. Whatever his plans are, they are wicked.

Walking alone, and not being on the run, feels foreign to me. I reach the Training Dome in record time and slip into a seat near the back. I press myself into the chair, hoping no one notices me, but of course Kassy does. She moves to sit beside me, an odd look on her face. "Are you OK?"

"Of course."

But her eyes tell me she can see I'm not. What does my face look like to everyone else? I can't imagine since I can't even describe how I feel. Afraid. Angry. Confused. Dead.

The training today is focused on improving the voting system in Greater City. As only the Greaters are allowed to vote for the Great Supreme, Supreme Moon has been reelected multiple times. No one in class seems to see the injustice of this system, and their efforts focus mostly on better polling locations, or the opportunity to vote via HELP comps at home.

The entire thing is absurd. Don't they care that

people are dying in Lesser cities so that they can sit in this fancy Training Dome and discuss HELP comps? Do they realize that for every extra portion they eat at breakfast, someone else is starving without it?

I press my hands to my eyes and ears, wishing I could block out this entire place.

When training ends, I quickly leave the dome. Seeing anyone—speaking to anyone—could get me into trouble. I hurry through the streets as fast as I can go without running, but it's not fast enough.

"Wait up, Hana!" Kassy calls. She reaches me, frowning. "Why did you leave so fast? You've got to tell me what's going on."

Tell Kassy? She's a Greater and telling her could definitely be a mistake.

She grabs my hand to stop me. People stroll past, some walking their pets, others hurrying by on their way to some place or another. I watch them go, considering what to do.

"I can't talk about it, Kassy." My eyes scan the buildings, searching for silver disks that let me know *he* can see me.

"Come with me," she says. She nods toward our building with a definite purpose. I'm reminded that she isn't as clueless as I first thought.

I follow her down the sidewalk, but instead of going inside our building, she continues walking. We finally reach the end of the street and take a left. After another block there is an alley. She pulls me inside.

"There are no cam disks here," she says.

I stare at her, still not sure what to make of her. "No offense, Kassy. I really like you. But I'm sure you can understand that I have to be careful."

She grabs my hands and looks me straight in the

eye. "You can trust me, Hana. They split my friends apart because we found the Broken City. We didn't know what it was—we still don't—but we knew it was something important, and they didn't want us to know what. I know how it feels to be watched."

The Broken City. I had almost forgotten about it. Kassy has information that I can use.

"They assigned me a guard to keep me in line," I explain. "And then they punished him to warn me when I wasn't doing everything they wanted."

She nods. "That's no surprise."

"Do you mean this happens often? To me, to you? Why doesn't anyone stop it?" Greater City is so messed up and no one seems to mind.

"We can't stop it," she says. "There's nothing we can do."

"That's not true, Kassy. There is always hope." The words come out harshly, and she draws back. I lick my lips and take a deep breath. "I'm sorry. I do believe we can change things, though. I do." But the idea of deliverance seems as far away as Middle City 3.

She studies me for long moments and finally nods. "I'll help you."

What little hope is still alive in me flutters and blossoms. "You will?"

"Yes."

I need to tell her why I'm doing it. She needs to understand all of the areas where we are being oppressed. "Kassy, have you ever heard of God?"

Kassy soaks in every word I say more quickly than I can believe. I hadn't trusted nearly so easily. She promises to help me, though, and her help is something I can definitely use.

We take separate routes home so we won't seem

suspicious. I stop at one of the public comps, reminded of the trick Kassy gave me earlier about disabling the security features. Now is as good a time as any since I want to give Kassy a good head start. Taking care to stay out of view of the tiny cam at the top of the box, I tap the screen and watch it come to life. When it loads, I tap the circle at the bottom right of the screen and it brings up a security box. I tap in the code Kassy gave me.

Cam disabled appears on screen. I smile.

I press the *directions* box. It brings up a myriad of options, and as it loads I glance at the buildings around me. One cam disk is mounted to my right, but it isn't pointing in my direction. Another disk is situated across the street, but the HELP comp itself blocks me from its view.

I study the maps in front of me, noting that the area to the southwest, where Broken City lies, is shaded in with green trees. They don't want anyone to know what's really there.

The city is much larger than I realized. I haven't seen nearly as much of it as I thought I had. The far border stretches for miles toward the east.

After ten minutes of studying the maps, I close down the screen, not even bothering to reboot the cam, and then I head toward my apartment.

I'm almost lonely as I walk. I hadn't realized how I'd come to depend on Guard Nev. With this thought comes new freedom, though. I can explore any part of the city now. I can learn every nook and cranny. I can meet others and find the people I most want to find.

My legs itch to head toward the lake, but something holds me back. What if Supreme Moon finds out and they punish Keegan?

I walk to my apartment and have begun eating supper when my HELP comp chimes. Keegan is playing at the concert arena tonight. I delete the message and almost delete the prompt that notifies me of his schedule. It would be easier not knowing. I hold my finger over the box. It lingers, wavering, and I can't do it. Knowing he is in town is connection enough. At least then I know he hasn't been demoted or worse.

I move to the bathroom and dig out my Bible from inside the dryer. My letter from Keegan falls out. Staring at it lying on the floor, I consider what to do. Keeping it could do further damage to him, but throwing it away means I lose the one part of him I have left.

His safety wins out and I take the paper to the sink. I run water over it until the ink is washed away, and then I tear the paper into pieces until it's no more than mush.

After I throw it away, I catch sight of myself in the mirror and realize I'm crying. The tears come harder now. My body crumples to the floor, and I bury my head in my lap. I cry for Mom, for Jamie, for Ava and Markus, for Guard Nev, and even for Keegan.

None of this is fair or right.

Finally, when all of my tears have been spent, I pull my Bible to me and open it. The pages fall to John, and I read, "In this world ye shall have tribulation, but be of good cheer, for I have overcome the world."

This is the answer. Only God can make the wrongs of my world right.

I stand and straighten my clothes, then wash my face and get a drink. Mom has been found and it is too late for her.

It's not too late for everyone else, not yet. I can't sit

in this apartment doing nothing. My mission continues tonight.

When I leave my apartment, the sun is beginning to dip below the huge, shining buildings that litter the skyline. A breeze blows, chilling me despite the warm night air. Citizens climb in and out of transporters, but I am glad I have always walked. It feels real. Alive.

My feet lead me to the lake, and I sit on a pier. A few boats dot the water, and the lights of the city dance on the waves. This lake used to be part of several lakes—the Great Lakes. I remember that from my schooling. It is still a great lake, but the other lakes are mostly dried up, like the Mississippi River back home.

The lights in the distance blink, too. Red ones.

I squint and lean forward. It's so far away, but I'm sure the red lights are in the sky this time, and not on a building.

A flying machine. It's something I haven't seen in Greater City before now, but my curiosity grows. Where did it come from? What is it used for?

Before I can stop myself, I stand and back off of the pier. There is a bridge in the distance, a bridge that extends across one part of the lake. If I can cross it, then I can double back and make my way to whatever it is that sits on the other side of the lake.

"You'll never make it," I mumble to myself. I know it's true. The walk is too far. I can't make it there and back before morning.

Still I press on.

The ground is rock and grass mixed. The scratchy grass scrapes at my legs and I'm thankful for the thickness of my pants. My feet ache and my lungs burn by the time I reach the bridge. Apparently it is still used because a guard station blocks the bridge's entry.

Two guards move inside it, talking and laughing. They stop suddenly and look in the distance.

Dust billows down the road, and I hide behind a bush as a truck rumbles to a stop at the station. It's white and shaped like a box, but nothing is written on the truck and there's no indication of what's inside. The driver climbs out and speaks with the guards. I strain to hear them.

"New recruits," he says.

Recruits.

Keegan's words about the prison come back to me. It's a training camp for soldiers, and the soldiers are training for war.

I step closer to hear more, but my foot snaps a twig.

Great.

Pressing myself into the bush, I lower to the ground and hope no one sees me. I hold my breath and refuse to even count. Footsteps pound the pavement, and I close my eyes as they draw closer, but after a few moments, they fade into the distance. One by one, I open my eyes, and then I wait. I stay that way until I hear the rumble of the truck as it pulls away.

24

Now that I know Mom is gone, visiting the other Lesser cities feels like a waste of time. What I want now is to get inside that prison. I stay up half the night trying to come up with a plan, but it seems impossible. The bridge is guarded, and even if I made it down one end, most likely I would find another guard station at the other.

Swimming across the lake is out. My only other option is finding a different way to cross—going around the long way. The lake has to end somewhere.

When the auto shutters lighten the glass in the morning, I rise from bed and hurry to get dressed. The faster my training is over for the day, the faster I can go back to the lake. Once I'm ready to head out, I open my door and notice a small piece of paper that's been slid underneath.

Meet me in the alley.

There is no indication as to who wrote the note. Can I trust it? It could be some kind of trap. But then I realize there is no one who would trap me in an alley in Greater City. If Supreme Moon wanted me dead he would just send me away, and surely he knows that if he wants to catch me doing something illegal, he just has to wait me out.

I hurry to the stairs and jog the seven flights down. After a few weeks in Greater City, I don't even get winded.

The door to the alley squeals open, and I stop short when I nearly stumble into Guard Nev. He paces outside my building, dressed in clothes that look like mine. It's the first time I've seen him without a uniform.

His face is a mixture of purple and green bruises. One eye is swollen, and two of his fingers are wrapped. One of his ears has an ugly scab covering the entire lobe.

I gasp. "Guard Nev, I'm so sorry." I'm not even sure what I'm apologizing for, but somehow I know this is my fault. Supreme Moon used Guard Nev's punishment to punish me.

He stops and shrugs. "It's OK. I've had worse."

I find that really hard to believe, but I don't say so.

The brick walls of the buildings on either side of us protect us from the watchful eyes of Greater City. The people whip by in transporters, and the only cam disk I see points toward the street. We are safe here. "What are you doing here? Did they reassign you to me?"

"No," he says quietly. "I'm here to help you. I won't be able to see you often, or for long periods of time, but I'll help you."

My mouth falls open, and I stare for a few moments before I can shake myself. They pushed him too far, just like they did me, only he's known and kept their secrets for years. Their betrayal goes much deeper for him.

"Thank you. I want to go across the lake. I found a bridge."

His eyebrows raise, but he doesn't question me. "There's only one way across the bridge, and that is on a transport truck. You would either have to ride in as a prisoner or a guard. If you went as a prisoner you wouldn't get to leave, but if you went as a guard you would need identification."

My hopes fall flat. So getting across is impossible.

"I'll see what I can do. It may be a few days before I can get what you need."

What I need? "What does that mean?"

Guard Nev holds out his arm. I see a small bump on his forearm, no bigger than a bug bite. "It's an identification chip. Every guard has one. There are certain check points throughout the city, as well as the city gates of each of the Middle and Lesser cities. Every time a guard passes a checkpoint, they are scanned and checked in. They will do that at the bridge, and you will need to be identifiable."

Guard Nev had his arm scanned the night I tried to get away from him, the night he was on Supreme Moon's porch with the secretary. I swallow hard and rub my arm. "Does it hurt?"

His serious face vanishes and he chuckles. "That's what you're worried about? You should be more concerned with the fact that you will be permanently marked by the government. Can you live with that?"

I glance at my arm and consider how it would feel to cut it open and take out the tracking device.

"I think so," I say.

"Then I'll help you. I have to ask, though, what do you think you're going to find on the other side of that bridge?"

I shift on the pavement, rocks sliding beneath my feet. What do I expect to find? Finally, I say, "Answers."

"Well, you should find that if nothing else."

There is something else I want to know—

something I've been searching for since I arrived—but I'm afraid to bring it up. Again I'm reminded of how brave Fischer must have been on that roof all those weeks ago.

"Guard Nev? Do you know any Christians in Greater City?"

He frowns, his eyes serious and searching. "I don't know."

I take a nervous breath and plunge ahead. "I believe in God, and I would like to find others who do, as well."

Emotions dance across his face as he considers my request. "I will see what I can find out, but that's as dangerous of a road as forged identification. More so, I think."

"I know." Didn't Supreme Moon watch my dreams just to see if he could find the Christians?

He nods. "If you're sure." He takes a step away and I stop him.

"When will I see you again?" I need this one connection, one friend.

"I don't know. I'll be in touch." He pauses, a thoughtful look on his face. "You need to use this time to prepare yourself. Learn the city. Learn everything you can."

This is where Kassy's help will come in handy.

I nod and he leaves then, leaves me standing alone in the alley. I can't get in through the locked door. I don't want to leave via the alley in case the cam disks are being watched, but I have no other choice. I wait a few minutes until I'm sure he's gone, and then I slip back into the regular world.

25

Professor Higgins discusses the city architecture the next morning in class. Three of the trainees will move into city zoning and planning, and they hope to rebuild some of the older, more unstable city structures. I lean forward. Maybe I can glean information I might be able to use in the future.

The city is built on an underground sewage system that was never meant to last and be used for five hundred years. As a result, the city is constantly shifting locations when old parts collapse and wear away. Most of the buildings have been remodeled and updated, but many of the structures are old and unstable. The hope is to construct new buildings as the city continues shifting. This would require tearing down the dilapidated buildings that stand in the way of rezoning, and this requires workers who are willing to get their hands dirty—in other words, not Greaters.

"What happens to the older parts of the city as we move away from them?" Kassy asks. It's the first time she's ever shown interest in Professor Higgins' lessons.

The professor's face freezes and I watch the wheels turn. He clears his throat. "The hope is to eventually rebuild." And he quickly moves on.

Kassy elbows me and mouths "Broken City."

Aha.

"We can bring in Lessers," one of the students suggests, drawing me back to the lesson. "They have to do what they're told. We can make them do the work."

"I thought we were trying to help the Lessers live a better life, not make them into slaves," I say.

The boy rolls his eyes at me, but Berry speaks up. "We can pay the Lessers with more allowances. This would give them incentive to do the work, and no one would be making a slave out of anyone."

I refuse to acknowledge his statement, but he's got the right idea. The conversation continues, but my mind stays on Berry. He knew where to find Mom. Did he also know she was already dead?

I tap the table in a quick rhythm. How did he get that information?

Professor Higgins drones on about the hope for a more prosperous future. He talks about the nation as a whole, not only Greater City. "There are hopes and dreams for a brand new society," he says. "Successful cities, perhaps more than one Greater City."

His words swirl inside my brain as their implication mixes with my knowledge of the way things have been done in the past.

These moves into prosperity will come at whose expense? The Lessers? Is this why Supreme Moon is so interested in rehabilitating them? It also begs the question—where do the Middles fit into this?

"If we had more than one Greater City, who would rule it?" one trainee asks.

"In the past, America had one great leader in the form of a president," Professor Higgins explains. "We will still be ruled by our Great Supreme. However, there will be leaders over the individual cities. In the Early Days they were called Mayors, and they looked after the wellbeing of their cities."

"They would be elected?"

"That's right," Professor Higgins says. "This would create more jobs, which would mean we would need more Greaters."

The class falls silent, and finally, one trainee has the guts to speak up, asking the question on everyone's mind. "Where will the Greaters come from?"

Professor Higgins hesitates. "You are the future of our nation, and as such, there is no reason to hold back. We will begin a process of new testing. These Tests will better identify those who have the most Greater potential. Some of you have already experienced this testing." His eyes fall on me and a few trainees turn. Berry scowls.

So that's what the dream test was?

I shift in my seat, uncomfortable with so many vengeful eyes on me. Professor Higgins continues his lesson, and the heads eventually turn away, even Berry's. I need to confront him, find out how he knew what he did about Mom, and why he let me in on the secret. For some reason, I doubt it was out of the goodness of his heart.

Training ends for the day and the trainees trickle out. Professor Higgins moves a stack of papers from his desk to his briefcase, but he drops them, scattering files everywhere. I move to help him, and we get the mess cleaned up quickly. He thanks me and I go my own way.

As I approach the vac chamber, I realize something—I'll be riding alone with Berry. He may be short, but he's big—much bigger than anyone I ever saw in Middle City. His sandy brown hair hangs around his forehead in a greasy mess. It seems to compliment his scruffy clothes.

I glance around, hoping to see a sign that can point

me to the stairs, but I see nothing. There's no other way, so I step into the chamber with him.

"If it isn't the Middle."

I scowl at him, telling myself it isn't time. It's not hard to refrain when the air starts whipping around us and we're both forced to stand stock still as we transport to the ground floor.

When we reach the bottom, I prepare myself for impact, which I've learned how to do fairly well. I don't prepare for Berry's foot, though. He sticks it out the second he regains movement, and instead of landing gracefully, I trip over his elephant foot and hit the ground with an *oomph*. He cackles and struts away while a few Greaters in the lobby giggle behind their hands.

Heat creeps up my back and explodes through my brain. I leap to my feet and race after him, reaching him as soon as he's outside. "What's wrong with you?" I demand, grabbing his arm.

He scowls and jerks away. "You're the one with problems, Middle. You don't belong here."

"I didn't ask to come here."

"You could have refused," he says. His voice drips with hatred.

"And be demoted?"

"Like that would have bothered you. You love them so much." A wicked grin spreads across his face. "You could have lived with your mom."

I lunge at him, fingers shaped like claws, and shove him against the dome. His head *thunks* the sleek metal structure and he winces. "How did you know where my mom was?"

"Hana! What are you doing?" Professor Higgins' voice interrupts my investigation, and his hands pry mine off Berry's chest. "Violence isn't allowed among Greaters, Hana. Not ever. Every Greater in the Dome just saw what you did."

I had forgotten about the see-through walls.

"That's exactly my point," Berry says, rubbing his chest where my arms had been. "She doesn't belong here."

Professor Higgins frowns. "Yes, well, you should be going Berry."

"This isn't done," I warn him.

He throws his hand up in a *whatever* gesture but keeps walking.

Professor Higgins turns to me. "What were you thinking, Hana? Violence against another Greater cannot be permitted. If a guard had caught you, it wouldn't have ended well."

I take a deep breath and close my eyes. Then, slowly letting out the breath, I relax. "I'm sorry, Professor Higgins. It won't happen again."

"I should think not. Go on home now. Get some rest and I'll see you tomorrow."

"Yes, Professor Higgins." I hurry away. The last thing I want to hear is more of his lecture. A more important thing to concentrate on is Berry, and what he's up to.

26

The city is booming as I move through the streets after supper. Transporters line the roads, and citizens move in and out of restaurants and stores. I act casually as I mingle among them, but my insides are anything but casual. I scan faces constantly, checking for anyone who might be watching me or following me.

So far, everyone on the street seems oblivious to my movements. My feet take me closer and closer to the lake, to the bridge. Traffic thins out, but I'm still able to move without drawing attention. Teenaged Greaters laugh and splash near the lake. They seem completely carefree, and I stop to watch them. They have no idea how corrupt their city is. They'll Test soon—probably this year—but they are oblivious.

One boy grabs a girl and kisses her right on the mouth. I watch, fascinated, when no one stops them. My cheeks burn when I remember how nervous I was for Keegan to hold my hand just a few weeks ago.

Putting them out of my mind, I continue my walk. I find a pier and take a seat, considering the path I should take from here.

Professor Higgins' talk today gave me some ideas. He talked about the old, broken parts of the city—the parts the citizens were always shifting away from. Kassy calls them Broken City. If the Christians in Middle City 3 use the dilapidated parts of the city to meet, then maybe the Christians in Greater City do as well.

If only I knew exactly where these broken parts were.

I watch people come and go, when I notice a girl near the restaurant on the street corner. She's my age, with unruly, curly hair. It's dark and cut short around her head. She wears the typical city garb of holey and unraveling clothes, but they don't look bad on her.

Something about her isn't right, though. She watches the area too closely. Her gaze darts around too quickly.

She raises her hand to call a transporter, and just before she climbs in, she glances my way.

Our eyes meet and then she is gone.

The transporter zips away, headed who knows where. I watch it as it drives further away, down the shore line, until it's out of site. It went the opposite way of the bridge. What is down there?

The girl's weird behavior has caught my attention. I unfold myself from my seat and begin walking. I'll never catch the transporter, but I can see what's on that side of the city.

The night sky begins to fall over the city. Street lights flicker on, something I never saw at home. Instead of hurrying inside as we would do in Middle 3, the citizens pour out of their buildings, going about their lives. How much freedom they have!

As I walk, I realize that I have freedom, too. I am out walking and no one gives it a second thought.

Everyone should be able to enjoy this.

The change in the city becomes apparent gradually. Buildings go from glassy and new to made of brick or block. Some of the bricks are chipping and lying on the sidewalk, but most of the buildings are intact and in use. Who lives here? Wouldn't the Greaters feel they were too good to have the "older" buildings?

Then the buildings begin changing to wooden structures. Some are kept up and appear in use, but the further I walk, the less cared for they are, until all of the buildings are crumbling.

I stop and gasp, looking out over the wreckage.

I've reached Broken City. How did this part of the city fall into such disrepair? Greater history tells us these parts of the city were used at one time. The first Greaters lived in these houses and walked these streets.

Did the sewers collapse? What could cause this much carnage of an area?

No one walks on these sidewalks now. I look around, hoping to catch sight of anything besides ruins. It must have been some kind of neighborhood. Houses line the streets, and trees and grasses grow up over and around them. The pavement is mostly broken, but not so much that a car couldn't still drive over it.

The place is a ghost town. The air is still and silent, and I shiver. There is nothing here but death.

I turn away when something catches my eye. It's just a flicker and then it's gone, but I definitely saw it. I narrow my eyes and push forward into Broken City. The flicker came from a ruined house a ways down the street. If something or someone is there, I don't want to frighten it away, so I move quietly, working to hide myself behind trees or old fences as I make my way closer.

One house away, I stop, straining my eyes to see

any evidence of something there. Another small light flashes in a different spot. The distance closes quickly as I dart through the overgrown yard. I squat under a window, holding my breath. Now that I'm closer, I hear footsteps. A floorboard creaks. Someone is inside.

Another flash of light blinks and I can't resist taking a look. I rise up and peek over the window ledge. At first all I see are shadows, but as my eyes adjust to the darkness inside the house, I see a girl. She holds a small, black machine to her face and the machine flashes again.

She moves the machine away and I hold in a gasp. It's the girl from the transporter!

The sky has turned completely black now. Stars shine in the distance, but the moon is only a sliver, and without the street lights, there is only murky darkness. Without my sight, I am useless. Whatever she's doing inside this house is a mystery to me.

Minutes pass as she flashes again and again.

A twig snaps somewhere down the street and I freeze. Curly freezes too. Her gaze darts to the window, and I'm not quick enough to drop down. Footsteps pound across the floor, and I hear the backdoor slam. She's running.

I sit tight for only a moment, contemplating whether someone else is here and whether I should follow the girl. Glancing around one last time, I run after her. She has a head start, but my legs are longer and before I know it, I'm gaining on her.

"Please stop!" I shout. My legs ache and I suck breaths in through my nose.

She glances back at me, but her steps don't slow.

On and on we run, past the broken houses, until we reach a place that looks like a city. Huge buildings, some with signs, line the streets. Windows are busted out of the frames, and glass glitters on the pavement.

She bolts across a field of pavement and runs inside an old store.

My lungs scream at me to stop. I put my hands on my knees and breathe deeply. A dull ache nips at the back of my neck, and my vision blurs. I can't chase her any further.

After a few minutes pass, I straighten and look around.

Was this where people used to shop? To work? To live?

This area is nothing like Greater City. It doesn't even look like Middle City 3 or the Lesser cities. There are huge block buildings, not skyscrapers, which line the road. There are wall to wall houses and businesses and schools. It is more opened, more relaxed, but its vast emptiness is unnerving.

The girl is probably long gone, but I can't help trying. I inch across the pavement until I reach the entrance to the store. The sign on the building says *Priceco*.

I definitely didn't come to Broken City for nothing. Taking a deep breath, I step inside.

27

The building is enormous, much bigger than any stores we had in Middle City 3, which were all small shops. I haven't set foot in any of the stores in Greater City, but I also haven't seen any that looked like this building.

Dust covers everything in sight. It's mostly empty shelving. Boxes lay scattered around the area, torn and empty, but a few look unopened. Clear footprints through the filth indicate a well-worn pathway.

"Hello?" I step forward, following the path. She can't live here because I saw her in the city. That means she comes here often, and most likely, others do, too. "Is anyone here? I'm just—" I pause. What am I doing? What if these people aren't the good guys? I could be stepping into something that won't help me at all.

I've just about decided to turn around when a shuffling sound catches my attention. It comes from further inside the building, from a place I can't see. The shelves block my view of anything beyond the front of the store building, so I follow the dim light coming through the window front to see the path.

"Is anyone here?" I repeat.

"What do you want?" When I hear her voice I nearly jump out of my skin. My heart thunders so hard it rattles my chest.

I take a moment to catch my breath. "I was looking for Broken City. I'd never seen it before, and then I saw the flash of your machine, and I was curious."

"Why did you follow me?"

I'm getting closer to the voice, but it's hard in the dark.

"A hunch?" It's a weak excuse, but it's true. "I was coming to Broken City for a reason."

"What reason?"

I squint into the darkness. "Can't you come out? I can't see where I'm going."

A light flicks on, blinding me. My hand shoots up so I can block my eyes. "Thanks," I mutter.

"What is your reason for coming here?"

"I was looking for people who believe." I lick my lips, hoping it is enough and not too much.

The girl is silent. Her face remains hidden in shadows, but after a moment, she lowers her flashlight enough for me to see her more clearly. "People who believe what?"

I swallow hard. "In God."

"Wait here." The light disappears and her footsteps fade into the darkness.

"Where are you going?" I'm suddenly trapped by the night. I've never been in utter and complete black, and I wring my hands together.

The seconds feel like hours, and after a few millennium pass, the footsteps return. The light flicks on and quickly finds me again, but this time she's holding the light so that I can see her. She isn't alone.

"Who sent you?" the woman asks. She's tall, taller than anyone I've ever seen. Her clothes aren't grunge, not like the girl's. They're not like any of the clothes I've ever seen at all—not in Middle 3 or the Lesser cities. Her shirt is made of a soft material. It looks comfortable and light. Her pants are made of denim, but they aren't work pants. They're almost attractive. Her skin is a deep tan color, and her hair lays in black waves down her back.

I stop ogling her and shake my head. "No one sent me. I've lived in Greater City for a few weeks, and I've been trying to find Christians the entire time. I was assigned a guard until a few nights ago. I've been exploring ever since I've been on my own."

"How do you know about God?"

They're so suspicious where Fischer wasn't suspicious at all. Of course, he approached me, not the other way around. "I learned about God in Middle City 3, where I came from. There was a group there, led by a man named Mr. Elders. He told me about Jesus Christ."

The woman's suspicious gaze lets up some, but her shoulders still seem tense. "Follow me."

She leads me through the long-deserted aisles of the store. We walk what feels like a city block before we pass through a door. Inside, I stop and gasp. Dozens of people cluster around a small fire on a concrete floor. I notice right away that most of their clothes are like the woman's, but not everyone's. A few of them are dressed like the girl and me.

"My name is Miriam. I need you to convince us that you weren't sent here to turn us over to the Greaters." She sweeps her hand around the room, indicating the crowd before us.

"I'm not," I say, shaking my head vehemently. "I was in trouble in Middle City 3, because my mom had the mutation, and I had heard about chemo drugs. I wanted to know why she wasn't getting them. My search led me to Mr. Elders, who told me about Christianity. The Greaters were watching me after that, and so when I tested as Greater, they assigned someone to watch me here."

"What happened to your guard?"

Poor Guard Nev. "He was punished because of me. I kept—tempting fate. They warned me to obey their rules, or they would do worse to others I love."

"And yet, here you are," Miriam says. She watches me through narrowed eyes. I'm not doing a very good job at pleading my case.

I swallow hard. "Here I am."

"Do you know who we are?" Miriam asks.

I shake my head, glancing around the room. Cots and makeshift beds are situated against the walls, and it's obvious these people live here at the back of the store. "Am I still in Greater City?"

"No," Miriam says. "You left it behind with the brick buildings. This is one of the Broken Cities."

"Are you Lessers?" I ask.

Miriam laughs, but it isn't a humorous laugh. Her face settles into a bitter mask. "We are nothing. Not Greater, Middle, or Lesser. We are those who live on our own. We are the Free."

What? I never knew such people existed. "How can you live on your own?"

"We stay hidden," she says. "We move around a lot as well."

"Are you Christians?" I ask, "Because that's all I was looking for." Offending her seems like a bad idea in a room full of her people, but I'm not sure even I want anything to do with people who are nothing—not Greater, Middle, or Lesser. It seems dangerous, even though the people in the past had no rank.

Her hard mask slips away, and she smiles slightly. "Yes, we are believers. We do our best to spread the message, but it's hard when we can barely go out in the daylight."

No wonder they can walk through the dark store without trouble.

"Will you teach me?" I ask. They owe me nothing, especially not when I barged in on them like this.

Miriam turns to the group. "What say you?"

28

They keep me at the center of their group, sitting in the middle of a ring of people. I feel like a trapped animal, one I'd see at the butcher back home. Mr. Garner often set traps near the levies to catch random animals to sell in the market for meat. We were taught early on not to go near the traps. Obviously, I never learned my lesson.

Miriam stands beside me now, the only person not sitting. She clears her throat and begins.

"Two hundred years ago, when the wars ended and the enemies left, the people who stepped forward to lead our nation had to think of a way to make things work. They had many, many people to care for, and most of them had nothing to offer. They were weak, maimed, poor, old. Those who were healthy and able stepped forward to lead. They divided the people into groups according to how much they could contribute—those who were healthy and strong became the Greaters, though they didn't call themselves that. Back then they were noble people, truly concerned with helping the masses. The next group was those who could contribute something, but perhaps not at the same level. They had land to offer, or services, even if they weren't strictly necessary services. They became the Middles. The last group was the Lessers. They were the elderly, the injured, and the dying. They were the widows with children to feed, or the people with illness. The leaders vowed to help this group and provide for them, since they couldn't provide for themselves."

The people in the storeroom sit quietly. They must know this story, but the few of us from Greater City haven't heard it before, and we sit eagerly, soaking up every word of this alleged history that we've never been told.

In school, my teachers told how the Greaters had saved us all, and I guess they did, but hearing it from Miriam's point of view is different. She doesn't make the Greaters sound like royalty—she makes them sound like everyday people who wanted to help.

I've never felt like I could be a Greater, but looking at them in this new light, I think maybe I can.

"Something was lost during that time, though," Miriam goes on. "The wars devastated something that had always been a foundation in America—religion. The churches had been destroyed. The Bibles. The hymn books and songs of worship.

"The Greaters were too busy rebuilding cities and a way of life to notice, and the Middles were too busy taking orders from the Greaters. It was the Lessers who clung to the religions. As generations passed away, some things were passed down and others were lost. When the Greaters started changing—when the children of the children were stepping into leadership—some of the Lessers realized the turn their world was taking. They saw that the new Greaters considered them a burden. There were laws being made that said they couldn't leave their cities, and the Greaters began rationing their food, water, and electricity. A large group of Lessers decided to leave their city before it was too late.

"At first, no one seemed to mind. The Greaters were glad some of their burden had been relieved. But then a new generation of Greaters came into rule. They saw the Free as a threat. This group of Greaters was the same group who decided religion had to be wiped out completely. Religion promoted division, they said, and they outlawed any form of belief. It wasn't hard to do, since by this time the Lessers were the only people who continued to believe and not even all of them. It was this generation of people who formed the basis of most laws we know today."

Someone emerges from the dim light and begins passing around a basket. When it reaches me, I take a piece of bread and mumble a thank you. It's the first time I realize I haven't eaten in hours. I momentarily consider how much time I have to make it home before I have to be at the Training Dome, but I push the thought away as Miriam continues.

"The Free believe something happened during that generation. Something changed those Greaters like nothing ever had before. We don't know what it was, but their laws were more harsh than any generation before them, and they have been hunting us ever since."

"Why do you stay so close to Greater City?" I ask. It seems like the worse place to be.

"They won't obliterate us here," Miriam says. "It's too close to their home."

"But they're shifting away from here. They're moving further east, and they put more distance between themselves and you with each new building they construct."

She considers this new information, as does the rest of the group. Their murmurs create a din in the room.

Miriam hushes them with raised hands. "We've survived this long. God will provide."

The rest of the night we discuss future meeting times. I tell her about the prison, and how I hope to get inside, and she promises to help me with anything I need.

"I can also get supplies," she says. "If you need something for your missions, you can ask me."

"How do you get them?"

She smiles. "Not all Greaters are evil."

It is well into the morning hours when I finally head back to Greater City. It's much easier to find my way the second time through, and this time I'm not travelling alone. None of us speak as we race over the rubble, and when we get close to the outskirts of Greater City, we go our separate ways.

I take the only route I know—the road near the lake.

The sky is barely beginning to lighten when I make it to my apartment building and hurry inside. I have two hours before I have to be at the Training Dome, which means I should be able to get a solid hour of sleep before I need to get ready.

My last thought before drifting off is of Keegan. If Supreme Moon finds out what I did tonight, Keegan will be gone forever.

29

By midday I can barely keep my eyes open. Professor Higgins rambles on and on, but I don't absorb any of it. All I can concentrate on are the things Miriam told me last night, and I want to get back there. I never did find out what the flashing machine was, or what the girl was doing in the crumbling house in the first place. How did the other Greaters who were present find out about Miriam's meeting place? It must have been the non-evil Greaters she talked about.

"Hana?" Professor Higgins' voice breaks through my daydreams.

I resurrect and give him my full attention.

"Did you have anything to add?" he asks.

My blank face must give me away. He frowns and strides over to me. "Are you sick, Hana?"

I shake my head. "I'm sorry, Professor. I didn't sleep well last night. What was the question?"

"We will be travelling to Lesser City 6 in two days. They are one of the more successful Lesser cities as an outlying city. Did you have anything to add?"

"No sir, nothing," I say. I'm fully awake now. The outlying Lesser cities are a complete mystery to me, and the thought of visiting perks me right up.

"Wonderful. I hope to visit each of them," Professor Higgins says, moving away. "At least most of them." He doesn't explain, and he doesn't name the ones we won't visit. But I have an idea, based on the files he showed me before the other students arrived for training. There are two cities that were especially suspicious to me—4 and 5. Particularly 4, which seemed the most violent. And 5 was the one titled "internment camp."

The other students may not visit Lesser 5, but I will.

The day finally ends, and I drag myself toward home and my apartment. Kassy walks with me.

"Do you want to come over tonight?" she asks. The look in her eyes tells me she has something specific in mind, but I can't bear the thought of staying awake another hour, not even for good information.

"I'm so tired, Kassy. Can we do it tomorrow?"

She frowns, her face questioning, but she doesn't protest.

This is good. She doesn't need to know I've found Broken City or what is hiding inside of it. At least not yet.

A sliver of guilt works its way inside my brain. Should I be shutting Kassy out when she's the one who told me about Broken City?

We reach our building and I push the guilty feelings away.

"I'll see you tomorrow," I say.

She waves and we part ways. Nothing ever sounded better than sleep in this moment, and I trudge across the floor to my bed. As I lie down and let my eyes slide closed, the HELP comp dings.

Groaning, I glance at the screen.

Communication Received flashes across the comp.

I could ignore it. I want to ignore it. But the thought of someone sending me my very own message is too hard to resist. I throw my legs over the side of the bed and hurry to the screen.

The message appears when I tap the box.

City tour, tonight. S.

No! The last thing I want to do is to spend the evening with Sindy. Besides, I don't want to go anywhere but to sleep. They must have noticed I was gone last night, even though they can't know where I went.

I climb back into bed for a few hours' rest, and I'm out as soon as my head hits the pillow.

The knocking on the door rouses me from my dreams.

"Go away," I mumble.

The knocking continues and the fog in my brain extinguishes enough for me to remember Sindy was coming over.

"Coming," I manage to yell.

She breezes in through the door as soon as I open it, but she stops short when she sees me. "Are you sick?"

Why does everyone keep asking me that? Too bad I'm not because that would be an excellent excuse.

I sigh and shake my head. "No, just tired."

"Ah yes. You were out late last night, I heard. Which is why Supreme Moon decided you needed a tour, so you wouldn't be out wandering anymore."

I force a smile. "Very considerate of him."

Sindy sighs and walks to the couch, her shoes not making a sound on the plush carpet. "Go get ready now. I'll wait."

"Of course." I hurry to the bathroom and splash cold water on my face. I do feel slightly more alive now that I've had some sleep. I change my clothes and grab something to eat from the food service, and together we head into Greater City.

"What would you like to see?" she asks, glancing around. "We've been to the concert arena and the lake. You've seen the training area. What else is there?"

I think about my options and a wave of homesickness sweeps over me. It must be the exhaustion. "Are there any houses in Greater City? All I've seen are huge buildings."

She draws back, her smile replaced with confusion. "You want to see houses?"

"I want to see families. Or does everyone live in one-room apartments?"

"Oh, that's all. We do have families, and they have bigger apartments. Everyone lives in the city." She shudders. "No one has lived in a house for years."

She says it like there's something wrong with a suburb.

"Let's see a show instead. I'll take you to the entertainment district."

Why did she even ask for my opinion?

She leads me to a transporter and we squeeze inside.

We arrive in no time. The building is different than the sky scrapers that rise to the clouds. This building is low and wide, like the *Priceco*, but it's much nicer. Lights dance and twinkle around various HELP screens built into the walls. Pictures flash across the screens, advertising the movies playing. People mill in and out of the doors, some laughing and some crying. The clatter of the people reminds me of the children at the park back in Middle City 3.

Beyond the theater are other stores. Some low and some tall, but all massive. Signs adorn the fronts of the buildings in bright, neon colors. No handpainted wooden signs hang over the doors like the stores back home. These ones blink, flash, and even play music.

"Do you like shopping?" Sindy asks. She glances at the stores. "You get to buy whatever you want, remember, as long as you're obeying the rules. We'll have to check with Supreme Moon, but I think it might be acceptable to take you shopping soon."

I hold in my laugh. It was a very nice way of saying I haven't done a great job of playing by the rules so far.

We enter the theater, passing through the sea of people. If I ever thought the streets of Greater City were crowded, I was dead wrong. I have only seen a small fraction of the Greaters compared to the masses congregated here tonight. They must love their entertainment.

A snippet of a memory passes through my mind, one of being taught the Lessers spent all their allowances on entertainment. It appears they had the social class wrong on that statistic. Big surprise.

Sindy finds a seat and we sit near the front. The production starts with a rambunctious musical number, and as the singers and dancers move on stage, I squint to study one girl. I'd recognize the smooth black curls anywhere. It's Lilith, I'm sure of it. She begins her part of the song, and she dances right past me.

If I can just find her—if I can speak to her for one moment—she might take a message to Keegan for me. She hates me and she always has, but maybe she won't hold it against me now. Maybe she'll help us.

The song ends and the actors and singers leave the stage.

"I have to use the restroom," I say.

Sindy nods, barely paying attention. Her gaze is riveted to the actors.

I squeeze between the seats, apologizing as I go, and hurry out of the room. Glancing down the hallway, I go right. It seems the logical direction since it's the way the singers left the stage. I pass the restroom as well as some type of gift shop. The hallway veers left and a sign hangs over a door. *Backstage*.

I take a deep breath and push through the door, steeling myself to get stopped. No one stands on the other side, though. People rush through the back hallways. Actors change costume right in the open, but no one seems to care. Stage hands shout directions to each other while other actors hurry onto stage. Finding Lilith in this chaos will be impossible, but I have to try, and I have to do it before Sindy gets suspicious.

Doors stand open and I peek into each one I pass. At the third door, I see the group of singers who just left the stage. No one notices me as I slip into the room. Costumes fly and the singers laugh as they discuss the show. Lilith is at the back of the room, changing into regular clothes, alone.

"Lilith," I whisper.

She jerks around, a frown on her face. "What are you doing here?"

"I need your help, Lilith." I glance around to make sure we're not being watched. "Will you tell Keegan I can't speak to him? They're watching me, and they've threatened his safety if I break their rules."

"Why would I help you?" she sneers, but her face is curious.

I grind my teeth and take a slow breath. "Don't do it to help me. Do it to help Keegan. You can have him,

Lilith. I sure can't. If he stays with me, he'll be demoted. Just promise you'll tell him why he won't see me again."

She pauses. "What do you mean they won't let you see him?"

Why does she have to ask questions? Can't she just help me? "I'm not exactly good at following their rules, that's all."

She watches me for a few minutes, but finally she nods. "Yes, I remember the things you did back home. Fine. I'll tell him, but you better not get me into trouble. I'll rat you out in a heartbeat."

I know she means it. "Thank you Lilith." I rush from the room and make my way back to Sindy. She watches the play with little interest in me or my absence. I settle in, but my mind isn't on the play. It's on the thought of Keegan being with anyone other than me. I close my eyes and try to block out images of Lilith smiling at him, of Keegan writing a love song for the girl with ebony curls, of them hugging—or worse.

I peel my eyes open and watch the stage with a pit in my stomach. And I try to ignore the fact that I may have just given up Keegan forever.

30

Maybe it's because I'm looking for it, but I notice the note under the front door as soon as I crawl out of bed the next morning. I feel like a new person after getting a good night's sleep, and I bound across the room to read the note.

Meet me in the alley.

I can't get my clothes on fast enough, and I pull on my last shoe as I scoot out the door.

Guard Nev paces the alley when I make my way outside. I grab a rock and slide it in place so the door can't close. "I didn't expect to see you so soon."

"I found someone who can do the procedure, but it needs to be tonight."

"I can come as soon as I'm done training," I say bravely, even though my insides aren't feeling nearly as brave as my voice.

"Good."

"Do you know when we'll get inside the prison?"

"No, but this is a solid step in that direction. It looks like the prison transports run on a schedule, but I can't get ahold of the schedule."

"Maybe I can help," I say. "I met some people."

He stops pacing, his eyes narrowed. "Who?"

"I found a place called Broken City. There were people inside. The Free."

His silence rings in the air like an alarm and my stomach knots. Maybe Miriam fooled me.

"What's wrong?"

"You started looking as soon as I was gone, didn't you?"

I laugh. "Of course. Did you think I would stop?"

He sighs. "I had hoped you would trust me to guide you in the right directions."

"I found the people, and they are Christians. I didn't get caught. It doesn't matter how I found it."

Guard Nev watches my face, and he finally shakes his head. "Fine. How can they help you?"

"Miriam, their leader, said she can find things for me. I just have to ask. I'll find out if she can get the transport schedule."

"Do it. I will return in three days." He turns to go but I stop him.

"Where do I go tonight?"

"Someone will meet you outside of your apartment after suppertime."

He leaves without another word, and I slip inside the building.

I gasp and freeze. A citizen stands at the foot of the stairs, watching me, wide eyed. She's an older woman, but she looks fit and strong. A small dog pants at her side, attached to the leash in her hands.

She wears the same grunge clothes everyone in the city wears, but she looks especially silly because her hair is curled and teased to stand several inches from her head. We stand in a showdown for several seconds before I take a deep breath and beg.

"Please don't say anything. I will do whatever you ask."

"I have to turn you in," she says, but her voice waivers. She glances uncertainly at the door then back to me. "Why were you speaking about those things?"

Lord, help me.

"I needed help finding my mother, and he was helping me." If she has kids then she might connect with this story. I can only hope she has children.

"What happened to your mother?"

"She got sick. She was sent away, and I wanted to find out where."

The woman listens intently, obviously considering my words. "I heard you speak of Free people and Christians."

I have no way of defending against her accusations. "Please don't say anything."

"What are you going to do? I can't let you go on if you plan to harm the city."

"I have no intention of hurting anyone."

She bites her lip and glances again at the alley door. "I won't tell, but if I see you doing anything else illegal, I'll have to turn you in."

"I understand," I say, exhaling in relief. I jog up the stairs so I can grab breakfast, and then I hurry to the Training Dome. What was the woman doing in the stairwell, anyway? I've never seen a single person take the stairs in Greater City.

Today Professor Higgins discusses what we can expect to find in Lesser City 6. Berry keeps turning to me and smirking. I want to talk to him again, but if Professor Higgins catches me, he won't be happy. Mom's file was not in Records, and that means someone else has it. Seeing as how Berry knew her location, I'm guessing it's him, but how did he get it? There's no way he has some secret access to Records.

I rub my arm, anticipating tonight and what will happen when they "tag" me. The thought makes my stomach hurt. I also keep an eye on the door to my right. Guards might charge in at any moment to take me away, but when training ends, and no one comes, I know the woman on the stairs kept her promise.

Berry gathers his things and heads for the door when I decide to make my move. "How did you get her file?"

He smirks again but doesn't look at me. "I don't know what you're talking about."

"You do," I hiss quietly. I don't want to draw Professor Higgins' attention. "Otherwise you wouldn't have known where I would find her."

He heads for the door without answering me.

Oh no, he's not getting off the hook that easily. I stay right on his heels. "Tell me how you got it. What's your issue with me? I've never done anything to get in your way."

He stops at the vac chamber and spins to me. His face has transformed from egocentric to angry. His eyes flash. "You've done everything to get in my way. When I tested I was told I was the favorite to work directly under Supreme Moon. As far as I knew that was exactly what should have happened, at least until you showed up. Then I hear a new student is training alone with Professor Higgins, and she's eating brunch every week with the Great Supreme. I don't know how you did it, or why, but I won't let you steal my place in society."

I draw back with a bark of a laugh. "Steal your place? I never asked to come here. In fact, I've done just about everything I could manage to get demoted. I don't know why I'm here anymore than you do."

The vac chamber opens up and we step inside. I stand as far away as possible so he can't trip me this time, but it doesn't matter because as soon as we land he bolts from the chamber and out the door.

He didn't answer my questions, but he admitted he was targeting me for a reason. At least now I know what it is.

31

I avoid Kassy after training. I almost feel guilty for it—she wants to help, after all—but letting her in on the secrets of Broken City won't do her any good just yet. And she definitely doesn't need to be anywhere near me when I leave with Guard Nev's contact.

The food service has left a meal for me, as usual. I scarf it down and am about to go wait on the sidewalk when the HELP comp dings. It's probably a notification for Keegan's upcoming playing schedule.

Please let it be a notification for Keegan's playing schedule.

I hover at the door, not sure if I should check it, but the allure wins out. I jog to the screen.

Communication Received flashes on the screen.

I tap the box and a message pops up. *Supreme Moon approved a shopping trip! I'll be by in a bit. S.*

Panic rises in me and I glance around like the answer will be flashing on the ceiling. What am I supposed to do now? How am I going to pull this off? Guard Nev's contact will arrive any minute to lead me to my procedure. Guard Nev said it had to be tonight.

Sindy's presence will definitely put a stop to that, and getting into the prison is more important than anything else, at this point. I consider leaving before she arrives and saying I didn't get the message, but they'll see through that as soon as they check the files on my HELP comp.

I throw my head back and groan. I'm stuck with Sindy for the night, and I won't be able to get my identification. Guard Nev won't be happy, and he won't even find out for three more days.

Sindy arrives within the half hour. I pretend I'm excited to go shopping, and as we exit the building I glance around casually for anyone who seems to be waiting. There's no one who looks out of place.

We climb into a transporter and it whips us away to the shopping district.

Once again the lights and glamour take my breath away. On the large marquis above the theater, an advertisement flashes for the same show we saw last night. Lilith will probably sing in each performance. Would she take more messages to Keegan?

I dismiss the idea immediately. She barely wanted to take the first message.

The masses are herded down the sidewalks by flashing signs and rope fences. Most of them keep their gazes on the HELP comps that line the walls.

Supreme Moon has them in the palm of his hand. He controls whatever plays on the HELP comps which means he controls whatever goes into these people's brains. They're like sheep being led to the slaughter.

Sindy takes me inside a store and I try to appear interested. Mostly the clothes look the same to me, except they have unimaginably bright colors here, ones we never had in Middle City 3. I choose a pair of coral pants—they have a hole in each knee—and a bright, yellow, knit top. It's cute, in an odd sort of way. Sindy picks out a few more outfits for me to try. I model them for her and she oohs and ahhs over me, almost like we're real friends.

We're not.

An ache in my heart reminds me that Jamie should be here, not Sindy. Instead, we've been separated by miles and social classes. What is Jamie's life like now? Which Lesser City is her home? Maybe she was sent to one of the outlying cities. It's possible I could find her in 6.

Sindy teaches me how to purchase items using my own personal ID. This allows the government to keep track of what I buy, and it allows them to put a freeze on my purchasing power if I don't follow their rules. The evening passes quickly, and I begin to hope that we'll get home before Guard Nev's contact gives up on me.

Sindy calls a transporter and we climb inside.

"I would call that a success," she says, grinning like she really did have a good time. She's only doing what she's been trained to do. She's a mindless slave to Supreme Moon's teachings.

I almost feel sorry for her, but not quite.

We arrive at my apartment and I climb out. She waves as she pulls away in the transporter, and as soon as she's gone, I turn to search for Guard Nev's contact. I even sprint to the corner of the building to check the alley, but it's useless. No one's in sight.

All hope isn't lost, though, at least not yet. I hurry to the elevator to see if there were any notes slipped under my door. The floor is clean when I enter, and I can't stop my disappointment. I hang the new clothes in my closet and settle in for the night. Nothing is going the way it was supposed to.

Mom is dead. Fischer is gone. Even the trainees at the dome hate me. Supreme Moon is keeping me occupied every second of the day, and I don't have time to find the answers I need.

Frustrated tears burn my eyes, and I move to the HELP comp to turn on Keegan's music.

They may be able to keep me from seeing him in person, but this is a part they haven't taken away, at least not yet. The music gives me an idea. I quickly tap over to the entertainment pages and search for Lilith Winters. Her name pops up along with a schedule of performances. She'll be at the theater every night this week, just as I suspected. I store the information away for later. Maybe she'll find more kindness somewhere in her cold heart.

The next morning, we move to load up for our tour of Lesser City 6. I tried asking why we were skipping Lesser 4, but Professor Higgins blew off my question and changed the subject. Kassy was the only one who would talk about it. She said she'd heard Lesser 4 was where they sent all the true criminals— the thieves, murderers, and rapists.

I'm glad we're skipping that one.

We reach the loading dock and everyone stops in surprise. At first we're all quiet, but then several of the students cheer. Instead of loading onto a bus, we will be riding in a transporter. But this isn't just any transporter—it is huge, and it will fly.

My legs shake as I climb on board, and I practically fall into the first seat I come to, but just as I buckle in, Berry stops at my side.

His shoulders are tense, and his jaw works back and forth. "Would you sit in the back with me?"

I'm tempted to reject him, but his serious face stops me. I stand without question and follow him to the back. He doesn't speak as the transporter lifts off and we head out of Greater City, but once we're well on our way, and everyone else is occupied, he turns to me and speaks in a low voice. "What did you mean when you said you were trying to get demoted?"

I close my eyes and take a deep breath. It's not only because I said way too much to him yesterday, it's also because the realization that I'm *flying* above the earth has me scared to death. "I'm not trying to get demoted, but the things I've done should have gotten me there."

"Were you caught?"

I swallow hard. "Multiple times."

His eyes narrow and he turns away. Moments tick away and he finally looks back at me. "My dad took your mom's file. He told me to find a way to make you go away. I can see now that's not going to happen."

"Who is your dad?" I ask. I don't know anyone in Greater City, and I can't imagine why anyone's father would want to make me go away. The fact that he knows anything about me makes my skin creep.

"He's the Head of the Guard. He controls which guards work in which city."

"Why would he want me gone?"

"I already told you. I was supposed to be where you sit, but for some reason Supreme Moon has decided the Lessers are his most important project for the time being."

"Why are you telling me this?"

Berry frowns. "Because we have a mutual problem. You don't want to be here and they're making you stay."

"I still don't understand how that's your problem."

"I want you gone." He says it so casually, like it should be obvious, and that it's a perfectly normal thing to admit to someone.

"So, what?" I ask, annoyed. "You're going to help me get demoted?"

His gaze moves to the nothingness over my shoulder, but he shakes his head. "No, that won't work." He looks back to me. "You met an old woman in your building yesterday. She said you were hoping to get inside the prison."

My mouth drops open and I glance around to see if anyone heard him. "You know about the prison?" I choose to ignore the fact that he must have sent the woman.

"My dad's the Head of the Guard," he reminds me.

I take a deep breath and think this through. If his dad is Head of the Guard, then he is military. He may have known Mom. I push the thought aside and focus on the present. "Can you help me get inside?"

"Maybe, maybe not, but I can try. If you get caught, though, it won't be good. You'd either be sent to 4, or you'd be kept here forever."

His words hold a foreboding that leaves me suddenly chilled. I shiver and wrap my arms around my waist. "What do you mean?"

"Lesser 4 is where they send the lawbreakers. You don't want to go there. But if they made you stay, it would be worse. You'd be one of the mindless."

So Kassy was right about 4. And it doesn't take much to figure out what the mindless are. He doesn't have to tell me about the pills.

"I won't get caught," I say. "I just need to know what's going on there. Why are the people being sent there? Why do they have flying machines? Don't you ever wonder about the way this country is run? There are too many lies."

"Who cares? The people are happy and healthy. They don't need to worry about all the truths that the Greaters have to deal with. They *couldn't* handle it all."

"They deserve to make that decision for themselves."

He doesn't respond and I finally turn away. We make the rest of the ride in silence. Berry knows more than I ever would have guessed, but he hasn't come to the same conclusions I did. I realize for the first time that, even in the face of truth, some are going to choose to not believe.

32

Lesser City 6 is nothing like the other Lesser cities we've seen so far. In fact, it's nothing like any of the cities I've seen, period—Greater, Middle, or Lesser.

Farm land stretches out for mile after eternal mile. Two cities lay in view—one free and the other behind a wall.

"What do you think that means?"

Berry glances out the window as we prepare to land. "One is Greater and the other is Lesser."

I frown, taking in the truth of his statement. Professor Higgins' earlier statements come to mind. Supreme Moon wants to create other Greater cities. It looks like he's already done that, only most people don't know it. Why is he choosing to let us in on his secret?

"Did you know about the other Lesser cities?" It never occurred to me to ask before now, but I never knew about them. Did Berry?

"No."

"Doesn't this seem strange to you?" His nonchalance irritates me to my core.

He shrugs. "It's like I said before. Everyone doesn't need to know everything."

We unload from the transporter inside the free city. People mill about. Most of them are doing hard labor. Many of them are young. These Greaters have probably never stepped foot inside of Greater City.

Have they ever even tested? They seem a different breed than the other Greaters who arrived with me. They're as different as their city—they come and go as free citizens, but there are no cam disks, no zooming transporters, no HELP comps lining their streets.

Everything here is perfectly proportional. Each house is the same, each lawn is the same. Every store is the same size and every street seems measured and mapped out to specific blueprints.

This city is new. It's not like Greater City at all, which is built on the crumbling old city. It's not flashy or boisterous. In fact, it's completely opposite from Greater City—it's quaint. This city was built here, and for a purpose.

Two questions stand out in my mind: where did these people come from and why are they here?

An older man steps forward. This man is in charge, I can feel it. Even his stature screams power. "Welcome!" he booms. "I'm General Funchess. I'm pleased to show you around."

Professor Higgins quickly steps forward and thanks the general, then we follow him as he shows us their stores and restaurants, their schools and their homes.

Once we've finished touring the Greater City— even though it's never called that—Professor Higgins clears his throat. "May we see the Lessers now? That is why we came, after all."

General Funchess pauses, his eyebrows drawn, his lips set in a straight line. He watches us all, taking in our faces, gauging us. "You must understand that ours is a delicate situation."

"Is there a problem?" Professor Higgins asks. He doesn't seem flustered or put off by General Funchess' odd behavior.

The general's nostrils flare and he takes a deep breath. "The issue is, quite frankly, that the 'Lessers' as you call them, don't see themselves that way. They see themselves as a free people, working to provide clothing and food for themselves and their tight-knit community."

I frown as I take in his words. Clothing and food? Now I glance at the city—the free city. I don't remember one vegetable garden, one factory, one cattle farm. The Lessers don't see themselves as Lessers because they don't know they are such. They are walled in, and they think they are free, but they're not.

My stomach churns as I realize the depth of corruption. I press my eyes closed and try to pretend I didn't just hear what I know I heard. Supreme Moon has already enslaved the Lessers. These people are in need of deliverance and they don't even know it.

Professor Higgins isn't put off by his words. "What does this mean, General? Tell us exactly what you need from us, and you will have it. We are at your mercy."

This seems to relieve whatever fears General Funchess has. "You can't speak to them. They can't be aware of the things that go on outside of their walls."

I look around, hoping to see the disgust on other trainees' faces, but none of them are upset, not even Kassy. Have they all been totally brainwashed?

Professor Higgins nods quickly. "We can do that. Observe and don't speak."

General Funchess smiles, his relief evident. "Wonderful. Then we will load onto the trucks and head that way." He speaks into some kind of radio and tells them of our coming arrival at the "work camps", as he calls them. We load onto the trucks and begin the drive over a paved road through the trees, toward the wall.

"What do you think this place is?" I whisper to Kassy.

She glances out the window and shrugs. "I have no idea. I never knew there were other Lesser cities. This one is different, though, don't you think?"

"Definitely. Why would they hide this from everyone?"

Kassy frowns, thinking. "I don't know, Hana. It's really strange, isn't it? It kind of creeps me out."

Just as I was starting to think she knew more than I had hoped, she strikes me as clueless again. She is a Greater first and foremost. I have to keep that in mind.

She is also a Christian.

The thought comes from nowhere, but it comes with guilt. I know where she can learn and grow in Christ, but I'm not willing to share it with her. Not yet.

That can't be fair or right, but I don't see another choice. Not until I am sure she won't be a danger to Miriam and her people.

Again it strikes me that Fischer put himself in true danger by trusting me so early.

At the gates to the wall we stop as guards identify themselves, then we proceed to the inside of the city. We drive between huge fields on our way to what looks like buildings in the distance. Cattle graze on one side and crops grow on another. This place supplies materials to the Greaters, but what are the Greaters doing here in the first place? The closer we get to the buildings, the more I see. Factory after factory rises up, and then buildings like I see in Greater City, great and glittering, rise to the sky. Behind them sit a few huge, brick buildings. They remind me of the dorms where Fischer lived back home. This is where the Lessers sleep.

The trucks roll to a stop and we unload onto the city streets. People mill about everywhere—the streets, the buildings, the fields—and they all look the same. They have the same dull clothes, and not only the same clothes but the same colors. They have the same haircuts. They are as similar as the houses and lawns in the Greater City outside the wall.

General Funchess leads us through the city streets. He points out the Official's building, the factories where they produce clothes, and the fields where they produce foods. The majority of the fields seem to be crops, and they produce way more than they could possibly need inside or outside the walls. The surplus is going somewhere else.

"This is where the people sleep," he says as we come to the last set of buildings, the dorms. "It is where the people eat, and also where the children go to school."

For the first time, I realize I haven't seen a single child since arriving.

"Might we have a look inside?" Professor Higgins says.

General Funchess pauses once again. He doesn't like it. He doesn't want us inside. The more we are around his people, the greater chance we have of blowing his secrets.

What would happen if they found out they were slaves? Would they revolt?

"I can't say I feel at all comfortable with that," he finally says. "This building is their home. I cannot allow anyone to invade their privacy that way."

His words do make sense, and I can almost believe the caring tone of his voice. Almost.

We turn from the dorms when I catch sight of a girl in the window. Her face is pressed against the glass, watching us as we move through the garden outside the building. Her hair is long and blond, straight as a ruler. She's younger than me, at least by a couple of years, but she's pretty. She smiles and waves.

I wave back.

This girl has a story. She is brave, and she is stuck.

I want her to be free.

The tour ends and we reload onto the trucks and then the transport flyer. We return to our own Greater City, but I have no new ideas about how to help the Lessers—not these ones, anyway.

Berry sits far away from me for the flight home, and even Kassy is quiet as we glide back to where we came from.

My mind is not quiet though. It is full of questions with no answers.

Again.

33

Saturday marks the third day since Guard Nev contacted me—three days was the meeting date. When he doesn't show up, I begin to worry. I sit at the table and eat my breakfast, going for normal as I check my communications on the HELP screen. If anyone is watching my cams, there's no reason to make them suspicious.

Guard Nev's absence can't be good, though. He had to have been caught. It's the only reason he wouldn't at least slip me a note.

Unless I'm being watched.

I grind my teeth as I move to the window. No one seems to be out of the ordinary, but that means nothing. I move to the bed and take Mom's perfume from my nightstand. I wish she were here with me now. She would know what to tell me. She always knew what to tell me. Once, when I turned thirteen and got my very first ID card, I worried that I looked silly in my picture. It was the first picture I'd ever seen of myself, and I didn't like it. Mom had smiled and patted my hair, telling me not to worry about how I looked right then. She said one day I would have a beautiful picture, and I would be important to the society.

Inhaling her scent, I remember all of the fun times we had together. She used to sing songs in my ear as I fell asleep at night. Her words always made me feel better.

I sigh and hug my pillow to my chest. I could use those songs right now.

Instead it is Keegan's songs that comfort me. I wonder how long it will be before they take that away, too.

I tuck the perfume inside the safety of the drawer, and I head to the Training Dome. The front of my building is empty as I step onto the street. The only cam disks I see are the ones that have always been there, and no one seems to be watching me. I walk slowly, glancing around casually like I don't have a care in the world. Unlike nearly a week ago when I noticed the curly headed girl getting into the transporter, no one here seems to be out of place. No one seems to be watching any harder than normal. In fact, not a single person seems to notice me at all.

A transporter arrives at the gate just after I do, and Berry climbs from it. "Wait for me," he calls. The transporter pulls away, and Berry checks in with the guard on duty. We walk onto campus together.

"Why don't you take a transporter?" he asks.

"I like walking," I say with a shrug. "At home we didn't have cars or transporters, or whatever you want to call them."

"Really?"

I don't know why this surprises him.

He steps closer and lowers his voice. "I heard my dad giving orders this morning."

A couple of trainees pass us on the sidewalk, talking and laughing loudly. We slow our pace as we near the shiny, metal dome.

"They're bringing a delivery of inmates to the prison in four days."

Four days. That doesn't give me much time, especially if I can't find Guard Nev. "Do you know if I'm being watched?" I ask.

His eyebrows rise. "I have no idea. Do you think you are?"

I glance around then back to him. "Yes."

He looks away, a habit I've noticed he has when he's thinking. "Do you know what you need to do?" he finally asks.

"Yes." I have to get to Broken City and find Miriam. She's the only person I know who can help me.

"Can you do it tonight?"

I nod.

"Then go. I will do what I can to make sure you don't have a tail." He begins to step toward the dome, but I grab his arm.

"Berry, why are you helping me? They will watch these feeds. They will see you talking to me. You're going to get in trouble if I do this."

His gaze is focused on the nothingness in the distance. "I don't think so. My father won't let that happen."

I want to argue with him and tell him that his father won't be able to do anything if he angers Supreme Moon, but Berry isn't one to change his mind so easily. "Thank you," I say instead.

He nods, still not meeting my eye. "Don't think I'm doing it for you, though. I have your ideas. Once you're out of the picture, I will be able to use them to rise to the top of favor."

Of course he will.

I don't know what to say and so I say nothing, and we head inside. Berry is cold and calculating. He doesn't care about helping the Lessers. He doesn't care about helping me. He cares for himself only. For the first time ever, I pity him.

As soon as training ends, I gather my things to hurry home. During training I made a decision. I will not go to Broken City alone. I will not deny Kassy a chance at learning more about being a Christian.

God, please let this be the right decision.

I grab Kassy's arm as we step out of the vac chamber. "Do you still want to talk?"

She nods immediately.

"I'm not going home," I warn. "And you'll have to promise to never tell." The memory of the new tests comes to mind, and I inwardly cringe. What if she can't help but tell? I push the thought aside and wait for her answer.

"I want to help," she says. There is no hesitation in her voice.

"Then follow me."

Cutting down a different block, I bypass our apartment building completely. After a few minutes of walking, it hits me that we are too visible on the street, and I call a transporter. "Take me to the lake," I say.

It zips away, pulling in and out of traffic.

Once we're at the lake, I head west down the same road as before. It's then I get the feeling someone is behind us. I turn, but no one is there.

"Where are we going?" Kassy asks.

"You told me about Broken City," I say.

She nods.

"Well, I found it."

Her eyes bulge and she stumbles to a stop. "You found it?"

I nod quickly and tug her arm to keep her moving.

"Kassy, can I trust you? I can't let you go on if I can't trust you."

"Of course you can," she says. Her face shows me that she's hurt, but it's too risky. I had to make sure.

"There are people there, and they know things about our country. Things aren't what we've always been told. You must know this, especially after our visit to Lesser 6."

She nods. "Everyone knows that bad things go on. We just ignore it."

"But don't you think it's wrong? We shouldn't be lied to that way. The Lessers aren't anyone's slaves."

Confusion swirls across her face, but she doesn't say she disagrees.

"They are going to help me," I finally say. "And they can help you, too, if you want to learn more about God and more about helping me."

She doesn't speak for a few moments, but finally she nods. "OK. I want to know what I can."

Something snaps behind us and I turn. Again no one is there, but I'm sure someone is following us. The only question is whether or not they heard anything we said.

After a few more steps, we veer inside a house and wait. I press my finger over my lips when Kassy begins to question me. Peeking out a window, I see her. It's a woman, dressed in neutral-toned clothes, blending in with the nothingness around her. She darts in and out of hiding places, making her way to the house.

Her movements and demeanor let me know she isn't a guard. She has been told to follow me, but it isn't an official order. Maybe it was Supreme Moon who sent her, or maybe it was Berry's father. It doesn't matter who sent her, I can't let her follow me. If she catches me, I will be demoted or worse, and I can't lead her right to Miriam and the Free.

God, help me. I pray. I'm not sure how to stop her. I have nothing to offer her in return for keeping my secret.

Broken pieces of wood litter the inside of the dilapidated house. I pick one up and take a deep breath. Can I do this?

She bolts inside the house and I swing. The sickening thud makes my stomach drop, and when her head hits the floor, I lose what little food I had in my stomach.

Breathe. Breathe. Breathe.

After a few minutes, I rise on weak legs and hurry from the room. "I'm sorry," I whisper to her. She's going to have a terrible headache when she wakes up.

Kassy is silent as we dart away, but her face is ashen, and she glances at me like I'm a stranger.

The sky has just turned an orange color as the sun sinks in the distance. No one else seems to be following, so I continue down the street toward Broken City. It takes me a while, but I finally locate the house where I spotted the curly headed girl the week before. I peek inside, but all I see are ruins. Whatever she had been doing with her flashing machine is gone.

We make the rest of the trip in quick time, and we reach the *Priceco* just as darkness falls across the paved field. Staring up at the huge building, I pause. This is it. If I do this, I will never be the same. I will have a tracker in my arm, and I will either dig it out when I'm done or stay tagged for life.

What if Miriam can't do it or can't do it tonight? What if I don't make it back by morning?

This is the only way I will ever get inside the

prison. It is the only way I will see for myself what is going on in this country. I have to do it, so I push the door open to find them.

34

"Miriam?" I call out softly, stepping through the darkness. "Hello?"

No one answers.

I can't see in the inky blackness at the back of the store, so I shuffle through the aisles, hoping I'm going the right way. Kassy stumbles along beside me, so I reach out my hand to her. At first she hesitates, but then she latches on and we walk together.

"Hello?" I call again.

This time something scrapes in the distance. Kassy gasps, but I turn to my left and make my way toward it. "Miriam?"

"It's me," Guard Nev says. He shines his flashlight in my face and I sigh in relief.

"Guard Nev! I thought you were dead." My relief at seeing him alive and well nearly chokes me.

He reaches me and grabs for my arm. "Did you get tagged?"

"No, Sindy showed up and I couldn't meet your contact. What happened to you? You said you would come in three days' time." I look him up and down, like the answers will be hanging around his neck. His right arm is wrapped in thin, white gauze. "And what happened to you?"

"They removed my identification tags and put in new ones."

"What?" That sounds terrible.

"It was the only way I could ever go back."

As terrible as it sounds, his words still bring relief. It means Miriam can do the things I was hoping for.

Guard Nev shines the flashlight in Kassy's face. "Why did you bring her?"

I glance at Kassy and then back to Guard Nev. "She knew about this place already. She isn't happy with the way things are done in Greater City, and she wants to learn more about God."

His face shows his disapproval of my choice, but he says nothing. Instead, he leads us toward the back room with his flashlight as he continues to explain, "I was apprehended for being around you. They say there was a witness."

The woman on the stairs. So she told, after all.

"When they came for me, I knew that was the end. They were ready to send me away, so I ran. I got away from them and came here, to the place you described."

He was so close to being punished—again— because of me.

I take a deep breath and let it out with a slow sigh. "There's a new shipment of inmates going to the prison in four days—or three days now, I guess. We have to be on that transport."

He nods, not even asking how I know. "Come on. We have to tag you tonight."

Butterflies erupt in my stomach, but I push them down, determined not to be a baby. I've never done all that well with pain.

The Free sit around the room just as they did a few nights ago. Everyone turns to watch me as we walk through the room.

Miriam stops what she's doing and strides over.

"Are you sure you want to do this? Going into that prison will be dangerous."

Guard Nev must have told her my plans.

"I'm sure." Whatever Supreme Moon is hiding, he's hiding it there. If we're going to make any changes, it has to begin on the inside of those walls.

She watches me, sizing me up. Finally she nods. "Your actions could free us all."

The truth of her statement settles on my shoulders like one of the heavy transporters. I don't feel seventeen anymore. I feel like I'm one hundred.

"Do you need to be tagged?"

Her words bring me out of my self-pity, and I swallow hard. "Yes." My voice matches my confidence level.

She stomps away and begins barking orders for the supplies to be brought.

Guard Nev guides me to a back corner of the room. Lamps are set up, and some type of medical table sits beside a bed. Everything smells like bleach.

My heart thunders in my chest and I take slow, deep breaths. This is going to hurt and I'll forever have a scar to remind me of what it felt like.

Miriam returns to us and picks up a clunky, handheld machine. It glows blue at the top, and it has a trigger almost like a gun.

"What is that?" I ask.

"Carrier gel. It will carry the chip in your bloodstream without letting your natural antibodies destroy it."

She grabs my arm and glares at me. "Are you sure about this? If I put this chip in your arm you will never be able to go back to Greater City."

I hadn't expected that, or prepared for it. What

about my Bible? What about Mom's perfume. "What? Why?"

"You'll be marked," Guard Nev explains softly. He must realize I hadn't thought it through. Bad habit of mine. "Every checkpoint you pass will pick you up. They might not notice at one or two checkpoints, but after a few they're going to figure out they don't have a guard who matches your identifications."

"Besides that," Miriam says. "You will be unconscious for nearly two days."

I grip the chair sides. "What?"

"It takes time for your body to acclimate to the carrier gel, and then the chip has to find a host location to attach to. You will be kept here and monitored until the prison run."

My gaze creeps to Guard Nev. He watches me intensely. "This is your decision," he says.

"Why me?"

His eyes soften and he shrugs. "Why not you?"

I close my eyes and pray for strength before nodding. "Go ahead. I'm ready."

Miriam raises the injector, and that is the last thing I remember.

...

...

I yank my arm away from whatever is searing it, but the pain persists.

"Stop," I beg, trying to roll away. My head bumps something hard and I peel my eyes open. A wall.

There are no walls around my bed in Greater City. Groaning, I roll over to see where I am. Maybe they've sent me back home.

As my eyes adjust to the dim light, I take in the storage room in the *Priceco* in Broken City. Most of the people are now lifeless bodies as they rest in sleep, but a few sit in groups, whispering quietly. Guard Nev and Miriam notice me right away.

Guard Nev rushes to my side. "Are you OK?"

I attempt a nod, but really it hurts to move at all. "Why do I feel this way?"

"I'm sorry. We didn't want to tell you because I figured you'd rather not know."

He's right. If I had known how much pain it would cause, I might have changed my mind. Changing my mind is no longer an option.

"It's the carrier gel," Miriam explains. "Your body fights it until it acclimates. You're probably running a slight fever, and you'll have general achiness, but by tomorrow night you'll feel much better."

I put a hand to my forehead. "I don't feel hot."

She reaches out and grips my hand. "That's because your hand is burning up."

"Don't you have any tech meds?"

"Tech meds don't work against carrier gel," she says with a smile, "but we can give you something mild for the pain and fever."

"Where is Kassy?"

Guard Nev and Miriam glance at each other. "She's safe," Guard Nev says.

I don't like the way he says it, but I swallow the pills and lie back down to rest. I'm out again before I can ask what day it is.

35

Two days pass and it's the day before the shipment. I finally feel like myself again. The fever has been gone for twelve hours, or so they tell me, and I'm ready to do this. We're leaving today to meet the transport vehicles for the prison. People hurry around the store room, rushing and preparing. It's odd that they're doing it all for us when they don't even know us. They don't owe us anything.

Miriam has provided Guard Nev and me back packs to carry on our journey. When we leave the prison, we aren't to return to their camp. We have to figure out our own ways, which terrifies me, but her request makes sense. She has her people to protect, and if we return here we could lead the Greaters right to the Free's doorstep. That makes us a great danger.

I check the contents of my bag before I zip up—a Taser, which I remember the guards using back home, flashlight, dyno sticks, and dried fruits and meat, along with bottled water. It's enough to get us started, but not enough to sustain us for long. We'll have to carve out a life for ourselves, and Miriam suggests heading west. She says the Lesser cities in the west are guarded less, and the land is open and mostly free. She says she's heard that the people in the cities don't even know they're slaves for the Greaters—I know she's right.

Her advice is solid, but I have no intention of

heading west, even if Guard Nev goes. My family, the people I love, are here. I will stay and fight for them. I'll find them if I can.

Days have passed since I left Greater City, which means Supreme Moon is aware I'm missing. Is he angry? Disappointed? Scared? He isn't one to let things go easily. I worry about Keegan. Supreme Moon will want to take my absence out on someone.

I whisper a prayer for him as I haul my bag onto my shoulder and move to meet Guard Nev.

We should be safe enough on our own, at least for now.

The same can't be said for Kassy. According to Guard Nev, she panicked when they stuck me with the ID gun. She wanted to leave immediately, but they couldn't let that happen. Not yet.

Muffled sobs come from a closed-off room behind me. It's all my fault. I shouldn't have brought her. How many bad decisions will I make before I start to make good ones?

Miriam promises Kassy will be OK. She says they will try to talk Kassy into staying with them, but no one has an answer for if she refuses to stay.

"Are you ready?" Guard Nev asks. He wears a pack on his back, and he's suited up in his guard uniform.

"Yep." Miriam's people scrounged up a guard uniform for me. The oversized camos feel heavy on my body. I'm not used to so many layers, but Guard Nev assures me I'll get used to it.

"Circle around the south side of the city perimeters," Miriam says. "The transport trucks will load near Lesser City 4. Be at that transport. The contact has put your names into the system."

I bite my lip, only letting myself worry for a moment. How does the "system" work? We were given fake names. I only hope I can remember mine. What if it flags our pictures? After a moment, I let the fear go. This is the only way to make things better. We have to expose the deception for what it is.

Miriam gives Guard Nev a few more instructions, and I try to focus on what she says, but I know so little and they seem to know so much. Kassy's advice about getting directions on the HELP comps is coming in useful, and I try to picture the maps I saw there. Broken City lies to Greater City's southwest. We will follow along the southern border, making our way back east. That is where Lesser City 4 lies.

I swallow around the lump in my throat. If I get caught, that might be where I end up.

Miriam puts her hands on my shoulders so I'm facing her directly. "You are stronger than you know. You can do this."

"Thank you." The words are confident. Too bad I don't feel that way at all.

She shakes hands with Guard Nev then we make our way into the open air. Dusk is falling, casting an eerie shadow on Broken City. For the first time, I try to imagine what all of this looked like when it was new. Did it appear as bright and shiny as the new buildings in Greater City? Did the people smile and greet each other in the streets, living in confidence as the Greaters do? It's hard to picture it being anything like that, especially in this wasteland.

"This way," Guard Nev says, and we head southeast, keeping the sinking sun on our right. For hours we walk, our boots crunching across broken gravel and then overgrown grasses as we circle the city. The night sky is an inky black as we near the road. I glance in the direction of the prison and narrow my eyes. Red lights shine in the sky. The people in Greater City must see them. Do they ever ask questions, or has all of their curiosity been bred out of them? Has Guard Nev ever seen it?

"Look."

Guard Nev turns and frowns. He stares at the lights. "What is that?"

"I don't know. Some type of flying machine. I saw it back home a few months ago. It's what made me start looking for answers in the first place."

He stares for long moments until he finally turns back to the path. "Let's—"

A rumbling moves toward us. Guard Nev's eyes widen and he grabs me and pushes me into the brush. "Stay down," he whispers.

We keep our faces low to the ground. Bristles and thorns scrape my cheek, but I don't move a muscle even when blood trickles down my face.

An entourage of trucks rumbles past us.

When the road is clear, Guard Nev stands up. "Stay here. I'm going to make sure it's safe to move."

He creeps away, leaving me alone in the dark brush. I close my eyes, pretending I don't hear crawling things in the tall grass.

Low I am with you always, even unto the ends of the earth.

The memory of the Bible verse offers a tiny bit of comfort, but I don't open my eyes until Guard Nev nudges me with his boot. "It's clear."

He helps me to my feet and we continue to the side of the main road, making our way to Lesser City 4. If it's as bad as Berry said, then I'm not looking forward to visiting.

We walk for a few more hours, and light is breaking as I see the first hint of a wall in the distance. My feet ache and the pain reaches up my shins.

"Let's rest here," Guard Nev says. "They'll leave this afternoon, and we'll be there, but for now we need to sleep."

Sleep sounds good.

"Go ahead," he says, looking me over. "I'll let you sleep for a few hours, then you can take watch."

I nod, too tired to care. I pull off my boots and inspect my aching feet. Blisters burn my heels and big toes, and I pour a small amount of cool water on each one.

"Save that," Guard Nev advises. "It won't last long."

He's right. I put the water away, replace my boots, and lay my head in the overgrown grass. My eyes are heavy, and I know it won't take long to fall asleep. As I drift further away, I have one last thought. I am no longer Greater. I am not Middle or even Lesser.

I am Free.

36

The rumbling of transport trucks wakes me. It's early afternoon by the way the sun hangs in the sky, and I sit up to look around. The first truck stops at the gates of Lesser City 4, and Guard Nev watches it from his hiding spot.

"You were supposed to wake me," I say.

He doesn't respond, but I have to admit he looks much more refreshed than I feel. Maybe guards are used to less sleep than civilians.

"What's the plan?" I ask.

Guard Nev and I crouch behind the brush, watching the trucks. We'll never get inside the city unless we're on one of those trucks, but how will we get on without being seen?

"Do you see the way they slow down as they approach the gate? We'll wait until the last truck approaches, and when it slows we'll jump onto the back."

Each truck has a pedestal and metal handles on its back corners. It'll be easy to get on, and once we're in, no one will question our names being on the list.

"Got it," I say, even though I've never jumped anywhere.

Four more trucks pull through, and the one bringing up the rear of the convoy moves more slowly than the others. We inch our way toward the roadside, careful to stay hidden behind the overgrown brush. As the last truck approaches our hiding place, Guard Nev looks at me.

"On three."

I nod.

"One, two, three!"

I leap for the truck. My shin bangs the pedestal, but my arms reach the metal handle, and I haul myself to a standing position. When I look over, Guard Nev already stands on his pedestal. He nods in approval, but I stare in awe. How did he get over there so quickly?

The truck stops at the gate and guards from Lesser 4 swarm the trucks, scanning each guard's identification. They come to Guard Nev and me, and we hold out our arms. My heart stutters in my chest. What if Miriam's contact didn't get the information into the system in time?

The guard barely glances at us, just scans and moves on. Once he's out of sight, I let out a huge sigh of relief. I smile at Guard Nev, triumphant, but he doesn't return my excitement.

I swallow hard, remembering that we haven't accomplished anything yet. We won't achieve our goal until we're on our way out of the prison.

The truck gets the final nod of approval, and we are jostled inside the city. We approach a huge warehouse and are parked before we have time to think. The guards pour from the trucks, so Guard Nev and I hop down and join them. I clasp my hands behind my back, trying my best to mimic some of the others.

A head guard steps to the front of the group. "Each group of prisoners will be chained together. Your trucks are numbered one through five, and each group of prisoners is marked for a specific numbered transport. Once the groups are in your trucks, go over the manifests to make sure each one is there."

He finishes his instructions and the guards move en masse toward the warehouse. I step into line with them, but my eyes are busy scanning the warehouse. Could Fischer be here? Could Jamie? How likely would they be to send a pregnant girl to the prison? If everyone's suspicions are right, then Supreme Moon is using the criminals of the country to fight in some type of war. It doesn't make sense, since criminals hardly seem like the best choice for soldiers.

My stomach twists at the thought of war. Who are we at war with when we've never been told there were others out there?

I don't recognize anyone in the warehouse at first glance, and no one looks remotely pregnant. Just the opposite, these prisoners are skin and bone. I help hustle a long line of them out of the warehouse and into a transport truck. Then I head back to assist another group.

Once everyone is inside, I find Guard Nev. "Which truck do I get on?"

"I saw the master manifest for truck four. My name was on it, but yours wasn't."

Great. So I need to be on one of the other trucks and I have no idea how to find out which one it is. "OK. Let me see what I can figure out." I march away, a guard on a mission.

Swallowing my fear, I step up to the driver's side of one of the trucks. "One of these prisoners looks out of place. Has anyone checked the manifest?"

The guard shrugs and hands me a clipboard with a sheet of paper. "Go at it."

I smile and nod, trying to hide the immense relief washing over me, and I step to the back of the truck to scour the list for my name. It's not there. That's two trucks down and three to go. I return the clipboard and make my way to the next truck in the convoy.

No one sits in the cab of the truck. I glance around to make sure I'm not being watched, and I haul myself inside to search for a manifest.

"What do you think you're doing in there?" A guard stands at my feet, which are hanging out of the truck. He scowls and rips the manifest from my hands.

"I was checking the prisoners."

"I've already done that. Get out of here."

I scurry from the truck without another glance. I didn't get a chance to look at the clipboard, and now I have no clue if I'm on that truck. I bite back my frustration and move to the next truck, but as I look around for someone who looks kind enough to help me, someone shouts, "Hey, we're missing a guard on our transport. Where's Nita Kessler?"

I sigh with relief and hurry to truck number five. "That's me," I say. "Sorry, got held up."

The guard nods and hands me the manifest. "Hold onto this for me, will you? When we get to the prison they'll check the Lessers to make sure everyone's there."

I nod, clutching the manifest to my chest. That means I'll be riding in the back with the prisoners. I glance at them, chained to the walls of the transporter, and swallow hard. They won't hurt me. They probably never did anything that bad, anyway.

I look at the manifest in my hands, searching for my false name. It's not my alias that catches my attention, though.

Ava Huckleberry.

My head jerks up and I scan the prisoners' faces. The last time I saw her she was doped up on pills after realizing the Greaters were keeping secrets. Now she sits at the front of the truck bed, near the cab. Her head is downcast and she stares at her feet, or maybe the floor. Dark hair hangs in her eyes.

What if she recognizes me? She could get me caught. But worse, what are they going to do with her? She's tiny, definitely not soldier material. What could have brought her here?

"Let's roll!" someone shouts.

I climb into the back of the transport truck, but I turn my body slightly away from the prisoners. If I keep my face averted then she shouldn't be able to see me. Besides that, I'm less recognizable with my guard uniform on, hat and all.

As it turns out, there's no need to worry. Ava is so doped up on—something—that she never lifts her head, not even once during the two hour drive. The transport trucks have small windows on the doors at the back, and I stand as we slow down so I can figure out our location.

We're on the east side of the city, and I can just see the skyscrapers in the distance. We rattle down a small, paved road, the last truck in the transport convoy. It's a constant stop and go. The first truck must have reached the gate at the bridge, and now we wait for our turn as they inspect the prisoners in each one.

When we reach the gate, a guard opens the back of the truck. "Manifest," he says. I hand it over and he scans each rider, matching them to the names on the list. It's the first time I realize the prisoners have been tagged as well. I glance at Ava, sadness filling me.

She'll be tagged for life—however long that is. It probably won't be long. Guilt blinds me when I realize that I never told her what I'd learned about God. If she dies, she will die without Him. I quickly turn away, blinking back tears. For the first time, I don't regret telling Kassy. I don't know where she'll end up, but at least when she dies she will die with knowledge of God.

"Now you," the guard says. I hold out my arm and he scans me. He hops down and slams the doors, then bangs on the truck. "This one's clear!" he shouts.

After another moment, the truck lurches forward and we pull through the checkpoint. We must be on the bridge, and I itch to see what's ahead of us. Being shut in this truck is almost suffocating. The drive across the lake comes to an end. I feel the jostling of the truck as we drive over the bump in the road that connects the pavement to the old bridge.

Now we backtrack toward the prison, toward the place I saw in the distance from the restaurant in Greater City. It takes only a few minutes and we're stopped.

Someone throws open the door and I take a deep breath and step into the light.

37

Huge stone towers dot the corners of the fence around the prison. The fence itself is four rows thick, each one with its own tangled, barbwire defense.

Gunned guards sit atop the towers, watching us. I've never seen a gun up close. In Middle City 3 we weren't allowed to have guns. Those who tested as hunters were allowed one gun each for shooting game, and each bullet had to be registered and accounted for. I didn't know any hunters.

"This way," Guard Nev whispers. He stands beside me now and nudges me toward the guards gathering around a man who must be the warden. The man goes on to explain the procedures of the prison, and how to get the prisoners inside the first building to registration.

I look around, realizing for the first time that there are multiple stone buildings. The first one is the smallest, and two enormous buildings stand behind it.

This particular drop off is supposed to be short. That means I have to get away from these people and do some investigating without getting noticed, and I have to figure out how to do it fast. An idea formulates in my mind and I move to put it in play.

When it's time to take the prisoners inside, I step up quickly. I take one of the prisoner's arms, like I'm leading him. I swallow back the fear that my plan is faulty. This particular prisoner might be as useless as

Ava. He might be docile. He might be plain stupid.

He isn't, though. Once he realizes I'm not paying attention, he grabs my Taser from my belt, exactly as I'd hoped. He whacks me in the side of the head, and I stumble, pain shooting through me.

"Stop him!" the warden shouts. A guard races toward us and knocks the man to the ground, but since all of the prisoners are chained together, they all crash into the dirt. I tumble with them.

Warm, sticky blood trickles down the side of my head and I touch it gingerly.

"Are you all right?" the warden asks, stepping toward me.

"I'm not sure. I feel dizzy."

He growls and shakes his head like a bear. "They ought to train you people better than this. These transports are dangerous. Don't tell me it's your first run."

I shrink back guiltily and he huffs and rolls his eyes. "You're bleeding a river over here. Let's get you inside."

I glance at Guard Nev and he nods slightly.

I follow the warden into the first building. Electric lights buzz in the entryway. An information desk sits just inside the door behind some type of thick window.

"Taking her to medical," the warden barks at the woman behind the desk.

The woman glances at my head and her eyes widen. "Yes, sir!" She pushes a button that makes a buzzing noise.

A door on our left swings open and the warden leads me through. We wind through the small building which must be where all of their administration is housed. HELP comps dot the walls here and there, but

I notice something else, as well. Telephones. I've never seen one before, except in books. They were talking devices back in the Early Days, and they were connected by wires that could transport voices all the way across the oceans. Does the prison use the telephones? Who do they talk to?

I don't dare ask the warden. He doesn't strike me as the talkative type.

I drink in every detail I can store away, from the layout of the hallways to the people in the offices. Several women and men work busily inside, and I can't help but shake my head. These people are all aware of what's going on. Who are they? Where did they come from?

We finally reach the back of the building and the warden pushes through the door. A courtyard stretches out before us, and beyond the courtyard is a huge concrete pad. It's marked with a giant red "X" that's been painted on the ground. A sign hangs on the fence nearby that reads "Stay clear of landing pad."

The flying machines. This is where they come and go. My mind works to consider what this means. Professor Higgins took us on a flyer to reach Lesser 6. Is the war past the outlying cities?

I realize I've slowed down and now I hurry to catch up to the warden. He leads me to the large building on the left. By now the blood seeps down the neck of my uniform. It's sticky and mingles with my sweat. "Sir, do you think we can get something to hold over my wound?"

He glances at me and grimaces. "Sure, sorry." We stop at the check in desk, and he asks the guard who sits behind it to get a towel. The man returns and hands me the towel, watching my wound like it might drip on him.

"What happened to her?" he asks the warden.

I want to laugh and tell him I'm standing right here, but I keep it to myself.

"Prisoner got her. Can't believe they're sending newbies on these runs. I knew it was getting bad, but I didn't know it was *that* bad."

I press the towel to my head, using one end to wipe the blood on my neck. The warden jerks his head and we move on, but my mind reels. What is bad? So bad that is would cause them to send newbies on prison runs and make the warden call it *that bad*?

Supreme Moon's office comes to mind, and the day a guard hurried in to tell him about "dissention."

Maybe I'm not alone in my mission at all.

The halls aren't filled with cells like I would expect to find in a prison. Instead, each doorway seems to lead to large training areas. This must be where they train the prisoners to be soldiers, which means the other building is used for housing.

We pass a cafeteria first, then rooms with weights, and rooms with what appear to be weapons. The weapons must be something other than what they seem, though. Surely they wouldn't give prisoners access to anything that could harm the guards.

"Medical is upstairs," the warden says. "Can you make it up the steps?"

I nod but he scowls at me. "You aren't going to pass out on me, are you?"

"No, sir, I don't think so."

He gives a sharp nod and leads me up a narrow staircase. The second floor looks just like the first, hallways lined with doors and rooms. We pass a library and a room filled with blue mats, and finally we come to a room marked *Medical*.

"I'll leave you here," the warden says. "I have to see to the registration of the new arrivals. You'll be able to find your way back?"

I can't believe he's going to leave me on my own, which is exactly what I want. "Yes, sir. I kept track of which way we were going."

He nods and opens the door. "Medic Brown?"

I glance around the tidy room, taking note of the hospital-type beds and the locked cabinets on the walls. The prisoners get better treatment here than they do in the other Lesser cities, and maybe even better than some of the Middles.

The medic comes from a different doorway, and the warden steps forward. He tugs on my arm to bring me with him, but I have to force my lead feet to move.

My eyes are bulging right out of my head—they must be. Butterflies erupt in my stomach and tears choke me.

Fischer stands in front of me, as wonderful and glorious and perfect as ever. "Yes sir, Warden sir?" He keeps his eyes trained on the warden, but he must have seen me. He's clearly handling it much better than I am.

"This guard was careless in her stance and ended up getting whacked by a prisoner. Are you OK?" he asks me, frowning.

"A little dizzy, sir," I choke out.

His frown deepens, creating wrinkles on his forehead and around his eyes. "Take a seat. The medic will fix you up." He looks back to Fischer. "Send her back out when you finish with her."

"Yes sir," Fischer says. The warden leaves and Fischer closes the door behind him. He keeps his back to me for what seems like an eternity, and then he turns.

38

Slowly, ever so slowly, he brings his gaze to meet mine.

All the worry, all the pain, all the risks I've taken to get to this place were worth it the moment our eyes meet. I can't hold in my joy at seeing him here and whole, and tears burn my eyes. He smiles and moves toward me.

He kneels before me, and I remove the towel from my head so he can get a better look.

"Not yet," he says softly, pushing the towel back in place. "Just let me look at you." He fingers my face, my hair, my shoulders and neck. He's never touched me so much, and his warm fingertips give me goose bumps.

"Are you really here?" he whispers.

I laugh nervously. "Are you?"

His gaze finds mine again. "How?"

"I found an advocate in Greater City. He helped."

"I can't believe it."

"How did you end up here?" I let myself consider touching him—maybe I shouldn't, I don't know. But it's too tempting to resist. I brush his forehead, pushing the dark hair from his face.

"They sent me here the day after you were promoted. This place is much worse than we thought. I've been praying that you would continue searching for answers. I prayed you would keep trying."

Keep trying.

New chill bumps prickle my skin. "I dreamed you said that."

His eyes are questioning, but he doesn't voice the words. Both of his hands move to my cheeks. He rises up on his heels, his face drawing closer to mine. His eyes close and I stop breathing.

He's going to kiss me.

I want him to, more than I've ever wanted anything. I close my eyes and lean toward him. The whole world can spin out of control, and I won't care if only I can feel Fischer's lips on mine.

His forehead bumps mine and he sighs. "It's too good to be true," he murmurs.

The disappointment is immediate and immense. I swallow hard and pull my face away. "What did you mean when you said this place is worse than we thought?"

He pauses, still looking at me like I'm a freezing piece of ice in the drought of summer. "Do we have to talk about that first?"

No! I want to shout. *Kiss me!* But how could I ever say those things? And how can I even be thinking them when I kissed Keegan two weeks ago?

Confusion swirls in my stomach and I pull away from him.

"What else is there to say?"

He rubs his thumb across my cheek the same way he did on my front porch in Middle City. "How about how much I missed you?"

I smile and laugh softly. "I missed you, too."

"How are you?"

I shrug, happy to stay so close to him forever. "Fine, all things considered. I'm pretty sure I can never return to Greater City."

He smiles back, his movements slow and cautious like he's afraid if he moves too quickly I'll disappear. This Fischer is different. He isn't the calm, confident boy I met all those many weeks ago.

Some battle is raging in his mind—I can see it in his eyes.

Suddenly, his lips crush mine. The moment is so shocking that at first I freeze, but then it's intoxicating and I kiss him back, my lips moving over his in abandon.

I don't know how long he kisses me, but he finally pulls away. His breaths are fast and shallow, and he closes his eyes again and leans his forehead against mine.

"I'm sorry," he croaks.

"I'm not sorry at all."

We stay that way for long moments, and he finally draws back. "I guess I need to take a look at that head wound."

Head wound? Who has a head wound?

He moves to one of the cabinets, and puts in a code, then pulls out a few bottles and medical supplies. His fingers move lithely over my head, brushing my matted hair out of the way and cleaning then stitching the wound. "Does it hurt?"

I shake my head slightly. I'm flying right now. Nothing in the world could hurt me. "What is that?" I ask.

"Tech Meds," he says. "I never imagined such things existed." He puts some of the salve on my head and it cools my wound.

"They give Tech Meds to Lessers?"

His brow furrows and he moves to put the meds

away. "These aren't regular Lessers."

"What do you mean?"

He shakes his head and sighs. "I haven't figured it out yet, at least not all the way." He takes a clean towel from a drawer and dips it in water, then begins wiping the blood from my ear, neck, and face. "Did you do this on purpose?"

"It was the only way to stay here longer. They wanted us to get the prisoners inside then leave. I had no idea you would be here, though. If I had known, I would have found a way here much sooner."

He smiles and keeps wiping. His touch is so gentle. "Have you heard from any of your family since you left?"

Family!

"Fischer, I met your father."

His hand freezes, poised over my right shoulder. "What?"

"During training we traveled to several Lesser cities. In 3, we passed the hospital, and I saw him. I spoke to him, and he was worried about you." The memory of Lesser 3 hurts so badly that I want to disintegrate in the small chair, but I push those thoughts away and let him bask in the knowledge that I saw his father.

Fischer's face takes on that same awed look he had months ago when I told him why I wanted to help the Lessers. Finally, his gaze drops and he continues his work. "What did you tell him?"

"All I knew, which was nothing. I said I hadn't heard from you in several weeks. He asked that if I ever found you to let him know, and I promised. I'll find a way to get word to him now."

He smiles slightly. "If anyone can, it's you."

I smile back and he finishes up. He has information I desperately want—what goes on in this place—but I can wait a few more minutes. I swallow hard. "Now what?"

"I don't know. If you return to the guards, they'll prepare to leave." He tosses the dirty towels in a bin. "For now, I'll say you're dizzy and you need to lie down for a while. We'll figure it out from there." He moves to a HELP comp on the wall and taps in a code. A woman's face appears.

I've never seen this option on my own HELP comp. Speaking live to someone in a different part of the prison? It seems unreal.

"What do you need, Medic Brown?" the woman asks.

"The injured guard is dizzy. She lost quite a bit of blood from her head wound. I need her to lie down and rest for a couple of hours. Can you relay the information to the warden?"

"Will do," the woman says. She pushes a button. "I'll call him now."

Fischer turns from the HELP comp and sits in a chair beside me. "Have you spoken with anyone else, besides my father?"

I pause, unsure of what to tell him first. "I found my mom in Lesser City 3 as well. They said she passed away as soon as she arrived."

His eyes soften and he takes my hand. "I'm sorry, Hana."

I attempt a smile, but it comes out wrong. "Thanks." I take a deep breath and continue. "I also saw Keegan. He's a musician, and he comes to play for the Greaters. They put a stop to my seeing him pretty fast, though."

"Why?"

I'm almost embarrassed to admit it. "I haven't exactly been obeying all the laws in Greater City. I know, very shocking."

He chuckles and shakes his head. "Most people's dream and you manage to mess it up."

"It was never my dream," I say quickly. "They could have helped my mom. They could have left us alone, and I never would have done anything illegal." The words come out more vehemently than I mean for them too, and I immediately regret it. "I'm sorry, Fischer. I don't mean I'm sorry for everything that's happened. Ignorance isn't always bliss, and I'm not sorry I met you, or learned about God. I just—"

He doesn't speak, only listens. He's good at that.

I don't know how to finish, so I just shrug. He pulls me toward him and I lay my head on his shoulder. I glance up at him and take a moment to study him, to really take him in. His hair is longer than it used to be, but only by a few inches. His eyes still twinkle with the light, and his smile is still ready, but he seems tired. He doesn't move as easily as he did before, and a faint bruise darkens his right jawline.

"What happened to your face?" I ask, brushing my fingers over the spot.

"Maybe I learned a few non-compliant behaviors from you."

I laugh and shake my head. "Why did you end up here?"

"They had to get rid of me somehow, but they didn't want to 'waste my talents' on regular Lessers. They sent me here instead."

"And you've been here all this time? Ever since you left my house the night Supreme Moon came?" He nods and I sigh. "I'm sorry I got you in trouble."

"You didn't get me in trouble. I was involved in so-called illegal activity before I met you. You just helped make it a little more obvious." He finishes with the grin that I love, and I can't stop my laugh. It's hard to believe any of this is real. When I first came to Greater City, I was sure I would see him again, but as the weeks went by and things got worse, I had given up on the idea.

"Can I get up?" I ask. "My foot is starting to cramp."

He waves his hand around the room. "Be my guest."

I stand slowly, trying to keep from getting dizzy. My head does swim for a moment, but I stabilize quickly. Large windows line the walls and I move to them. The lake stretches out before me, and beyond it, Greater City.

"I have thought of you every single day," Fischer says softly. He moves to stand beside me and after a moment, his fingers intertwine with mine. Warmth surges through my hand, up my arm, and into my heart. I've waited for this to happen, longed for it to happen.

No wonder Jamie had a hard time resisting Easton last school year.

But a future with Fischer seems almost impossible. How is he going to escape from this place? And once I leave, I surely won't be able to come back. What does the future look like for him? For me? For Keegan?

Thinking of Keegan brings a flash of guilt, but I push it away. I can't choose between him and Fischer, not today, not with the way my life is shaping up. At least Fischer and Keegan have the promise of a stable future. Fischer will be here, tending to the patients, and Keegan will continue his life in Middle City 1, singing and entertaining the masses.

I will be alone, cast out.

You will never be alone.

How do I keep forgetting that? I pray a quick prayer for forgiveness and force myself to push the thoughts away.

"I have looked out that window and seen Greater City, and I've known you were there," Fischer says.

I smile, thinking of the pier on the other side of the lake. "I used to sit over there and look at this place. Maybe we've been looking at each other and never knew it."

He returns my smile and tightens his grip on my hand.

I won't think about our future, at least not right now. For this moment, I have Fischer. And that is all that matters.

39

We stand together for long minutes, gazing out toward Greater City and just being happy to see each other. Finally, I pull away from him and turn my attention to the rest of the room. I move across the space, fingering this and that.

"Your HELP comp is different than the one I have in Greater City." I tap on the screen and it glows to life.

"This one does research," he says. "I can type in symptoms, or almost anything I need to know and it will bring up the answer. It's especially helpful with patient histories or when I need to cross reference medications."

A question weighs on my mind. Should I ask it?

"Do any of the prisoners get the mutation?"

He seems to know what I'm asking before I have to say it. He turns his attention to the HELP screen and taps in "Chemotherapy".

Request Denied flashes on the screen.

At first I feel relief—they didn't help my mom, but they're not helping anyone else, either—but the relief is quickly replaced by guilt. How could I wish to deny anyone else the help they might need? The truth is the help shouldn't be denied to anyone, at least not based on their social class.

"What do you do around here for fun?" I ask, tapping here and there. Other boxes line his comp, but there are none for music or movies.

"There's no time for fun. The prisoners are always training, and during training someone always gets hurt. The rest of the time I sleep."

It's almost the same answer he gave me in Middle City 3 when I asked if he ever got a day off. I think the truth is closer to the fact that Fischer likes to work. I don't bring this up, though.

"I didn't see anyone training when I came in."

"They don't train during new arrival times. It tends to cause chaos."

Images of veteran prisoners taunting the new ones, or the new ones revolting, cross my mind. No, it wouldn't be a good situation. I point in the direction of the other building that I haven't seen. "Is that where everyone sleeps?"

He nods.

The HELP comp flashes and beeps and I back away. "Uh-oh. What did I do?"

Passcode required flashes on screen.

"It's OK." He types in a code and the flashing stops. "Whatever you're trying to access needs my approval, that's all."

I've had enough of the Greater's technology, though, so I move back to my seat.

"Can you tell me what you've learned while you've been here?"

He sighs and leans against the wall near the HELP comp. "New transports arrive every two weeks. The prisoners are trained in the art of war. They learn tactics, fighting techniques, survival skills—anything they might need in war time to survive. Some learn faster than others, but that is tolerated. They don't 'graduate' until they are experts."

"Who are we at war with?" I'm almost afraid to know. Will an unknown enemy invade our country? When will they come? And why?

"I don't know." I can hear the frustration in his voice. "I don't get most of the pertinent information, only what I need to treat the patients, but a flying transport arrives once a month. It's happened three times since I've arrived. The transport takes any soldiers who are ready for war, and they leave. Those soldiers never return."

Chill bumps race up my arms and I shiver. It sounds terrible.

"There are other Lesser cities," I say. "Did you know that?"

He frowns and shakes his head.

"There are eight all together. The outlying cities grow crops, raise herds of cattle and sheep, run textile industries, and who knows what else. Where do those supplies go? Who are we growing them for? They apparently don't benefit our own citizens."

It's obvious by the lost look on his face that this is all new to him. "I don't understand."

"I don't, either, but there's more. I found a group of Christians in an old, ruined town on the outskirts of Greater City. It's called Broken City. They call themselves the Free, and they say there are people like them all over the land. They said things weren't always this way in our country, but that something happened to change the Greaters. That was when religion was outlawed and things got tough for the Lessers."

"Are you sure you can trust those people?" He reminds me of Guard Nev. He's so used to being in control that he doesn't trust anything he hasn't checked out for himself.

"They helped me get here," I say with a shrug. "They even gave me instructions on where to go when I get out."

A loud ringing pierces our ears then stops suddenly. We frown and look around, but only a moment later, a din of voices fills the air. At first it's distant, but soon it grows into a roar.

"What is that?" I ask.

Fischer races to the door and throws it open. "I don't see anything—" he begins, but stops.

I hear his voice in two ways. One because he's standing in the room with me, but two because everything he said has been amplified over the prison-wide speakers. My gaze flies to the HELP comp. Whatever I activated on his screen broadcasted our conversation to the entire prison.

The shouting is more distinct now. Something breaks in a room down the stairs and footsteps pound on the concrete floors like a herd of marching soldiers. I shudder when I realize that is exactly what it is.

"They heard us," I whisper with a gasp.

His face becomes as white as snow and he swallows. "Everyone heard us. The warden, the guards..."

"And the prisoners," I finish.

He nods and we rush to the windows. Chaos has broken out across the courtyard. There are more prisoners than guards, and these aren't just any prisoners—they're prisoners who have been trained in the art of fighting to the death, and now they know exactly why they're here and what they're being sent to. They know about the Free, and they know there are others who are revolting. These are people who had already been exiled to Lesser City 4, have watched their loved ones taken from them, and who have been doped up on pills and left to starve. This new information is all the push they need to join the rebellion.

I swallow hard and clasp my hands to keep them from shaking.

If Supreme Moon wasn't ready for my head before, then he will be now.

40

Guard Nev busts through the medical room door and glances between Fischer and me. He doesn't question our relationship or anything he had to have heard over the speaker system. His face is ragged and a deep gash oozes blood over his left eyebrow. "We have to go. Now!"

His words kick us into action.

Fischer grabs a pack hanging on a hook nearby and begins shoving any medical supplies and water he can fit inside. "Help me," he says.

Guard Nev grabs another bag and we work to put in towels and Tech Meds.

"It will only take minutes for the guards to come," Guard Nev says.

"Don't they have their hands full with fighting the prisoners?"

"That's not what I mean," he says. His eyes are grave. "I meant the guards from Greater City."

Oh.

It only makes sense that the warden would notify Supreme Moon immediately that there was a riot at the prison. "How will we get out? The only way across the lake is the bridge."

"That's the only way if you're going to Greater City," Fischer says. "But we're not going there. We can go west. The land goes on forever."

My heart thunders in my chest. We're leaving and

Fischer is coming with us. *Thank you, God.*

Guard Nev nods his approval and we finish packing the bags. He takes one and Fisher takes another. We step toward the door, but Guard Nev stops us. "It's bad out there. Once we step into the crush, I can't promise any of us will be able to stick together. Get outside and head west. Whatever you do, head west. We can all meet up eventually."

The thought of getting stuck in the riot makes my blood run cold, but I don't have time to dwell on it. Guard Nev opens the door and pulls me into the hallway with him.

Prisoners have just emerged at the top of the stairwell. Their eyes lock onto us and it's like the calm before the storm. The hatred in their eyes is searing and deep. At first, I'm confused. We're here to help them! But then I realize what they see—two guards and the prison medic.

Before I have time to blink, Fischer has grabbed my arm and we're racing down the hall in the opposite direction. The prisoners don't hesitate and their footsteps reverberate against the stone floors. The entire building seems to shake

"Hurry!" Fischer says, tugging my hand.

"You filthy liars!" a prisoner shouts.

I want to scream out my innocence, but I'm too busy running for my life. Besides, I doubt the prisoners are in a listening mood.

We reach a different stairwell. "This way," Guard Nev says. He heads down first, but at the third step a group of prisoners emerges at the bottom.

"Back!"

Fischer shuffles backwards with Guard Nev and me following. We reach the top and have just enough time to run before the first group of prisoners reaches the stairwell. We pass rooms full of weights and exercise equipment and my brain goes into overtime. If the prisoners start grabbing those weights for weapons, we're all in trouble, but what about the weapons downstairs?

"Are there real weapons in the training room I saw downstairs?" I ask Fischer as we round a corner. The hallway is empty so far, but my lungs are beginning to burn.

"Some," he says. "There are Tasers and night sticks, but the swords are only for fencing and the guns shoot blanks."

Thank you again, Lord.

We round another corner and Guard Nev dashes inside an open door. We follow him and he shuts the door moments before the prisoners follow us into the new hallway. He puts his finger to his lips and motions for us to stay below the window in the door. The riot continues past us with prisoners beating the walls and bashing everything in their path.

"How are we going to get out of here?" I hiss.

Guard Nev turns to Fischer. "You live here. You tell us. How do we get out?"

Fischer's nostrils flare. This shouldn't be hard for him—he always has a plan. "The second stairwell we came to leads straight to an outside door. It's our best shot."

Guard Nev takes a long, deep breath and blows it out through his nose. "Then we have to get to that stairwell. It's only a matter of time before someone finds us in this room, and if it's not the prisoners it will be the reinforcements."

I'm not sure which would be worse. "Should we

wait until the din dies down?"

"There's no point in waiting," Fischer says, shaking his head. "There's no waiting out angry prisoners. The only thing that will subdue them is the guards, and we don't want to get caught by them, either. Don't forget, they heard what we said, too."

"Let's go," Guard Nev says. He stands and looks out the window in the door. "It's now or never."

I take a deep breath and work up the courage to follow him into the hall. Guard Nev opens the door and we peek outside. It's clear, for the moment. We rush around the corner and make a mad dash for the stairs. A single prisoner jogs up the steps. He pauses when he sees us, but the panic on his face turns to rage and he screams, barreling toward us.

Guard Nev growls and shakes his head. It isn't his wish to hurt anyone. I know him well enough to know that. But he has no choice. When we reach the prisoner, Guard Nev gives him a hard shove with his shoulder, and the man tumbles backwards, flying through the air until he hits the cement floor at the bottom with a thud. Dark blood puddles at the back of his skull.

My stomach twists at the sight, and I turn my eyes away. The best I can hope is that he isn't dead.

The door at the bottom of the stairs is in sight. It's maybe ten feet from us, but a small group of prisoners is coming toward us. They must have been drawn by the other man's screams. These prisoners won't be as easy to get away from. They each carry guard sticks, and by the looks on their faces I'd say they're eager to use them.

"Run!" Fischer shouts. I don't hesitate and I'm the first to reach the door and push into the outside. The scene stretched out before me stops me for a moment, but I get ahold of myself and keep moving. Guards in the courtyard hit prisoners with guard sticks, prisoners electrify guards with Tasers, and bodies litter the blood-stained ground.

"Go left," Guard Nev says.

Left is as good as any other direction. I turn left and head for the fence. Barbed wire swirls at the top of each row of fencing, but I can't let it frighten me. Scratches will heal, and I can't help anyone if I'm dead or caught.

I immediately leap onto the fence and shuffle toward the top. A bang echoes through the air and I freeze.

"Keep going!" Guard Nev says. He hasn't begun climbing yet, but his hands are on the chains. "It was a gunshot. It's the guards shooting at the prisoners. You're one of them. They won't shoot you."

A commotion on the ground catches our attention and we turn. Three men race toward the fence. Two are prisoners with Tasers, and one is a guard chasing the prisoners. I don't recognize this guard, and so he can't know I'm the one who set this riot off. As far as he knows, I'm helping. Maybe between him and Guard Nev they'll be able to fight the prisoners off.

I scramble the rest of the way up the fence, and I only pause for a moment before I barrel over the top. Pain slices through me as the barbed wire snags and rips my skin. I can't hold on for the intense pain and I fall from the top, hitting the gravel on the other side with a thud. I give myself five seconds before I force myself to begin climbing the second fence. It's only as I reach the top that I realize I never saw Fischer come out of the prison.

41

By the time I get over the fourth fence, my guard uniform is torn and bloody. My hands are raw, like the scrambled meat we sometimes used to buy to make stews with back home. My cheeks sting with sticky, bloody wounds, and I'm pretty sure I left a wad of hair behind on one of those fences. A few prisoners have also made it over, but they are much more interested in escape than in catching me.

I lie in the grass, moaning in pain, and I watch four men running in the distance. *Keep running!* I want to shout. *Go as fast and as far as you can!*

But I'm in too much pain to yell anything.

Minutes pass, maybe hours, but I finally gather enough courage to move. Pain burns through my entire body. Each step shoots pain up my legs. My back hurts, probably from each time I tumbled over a fence top. When I'm ten yards from the fences, I turn back. Two men are lying on the ground on the other side of the very first fence. Both are prisoners and both moan in pain. Where are Fischer and Guard Nev? I can't leave them behind. I'm nothing without them.

You are never alone.

But I feel completely alone. I need someone, so I change directions. We were supposed to meet in the west, but neither of them has made it over a fence, and the only other way out is across the bridge. I have to find them to see if they need help. Or because I need help.

My legs tremble as I make my way back. The grass here is uncut, and it grows in a tangled mess. The scratchy stalks brush against the open skin on my legs, and I wince with every step. At the first fence, I hold on just to keep myself from falling and I peer inside, looking for a sign of Guard Nev.

I see lots of guards, some standing and some not, but none are him. I inch my way along the fence line, scanning the area for a sign of Fischer. He's nowhere to be seen. I have to find him. I have to! I just got him back, and now he's gone again. It can't end here. I have to find him.

As I make my way toward the front of the prison, I round a corner and my breath stops. Part of the fences have been torn down—all four rows. A few bodies lie between the prison and freedom, but men run in the distance, making their break for unpatrolled lands. They're obviously unfamiliar with the area, though, because they head toward the bridge and Greater City. Don't they know what brought them here? But they keep running.

Trucks rumble in the distance and a cloud of dust moves across the bridge. The reinforcements are coming. I watch the trucks approach, confident for now that I'm safe. Most of the prisoners who are left are making a run for it, and the guards don't find me a threat. Unless I run into the warden.

If only I could find Guard Nev, I could figure out the best course of action. I'm useless going into the wild on my own.

I've almost made the decision to take my chances going back into the city when the chain link fence behind me rattles.

I spin around, hoping it's a friendly face but prepared for an attack. A prisoner lunges for me, fingers drawn like claws.

"Monster!" she screams.

Her voice is recognizable instantly. "Ava! Ava, it's me, Hana!"

Her face twists into a scowl and she snarls. "You're a filthy, stinking guard! And a liar!" She lunges again and I barely get away before she barrels into the fence. Her eyes are wild and crazed.

"I'm not lying. It's me, Hana Norfolk, from Middle City 3!"

My face burns as my mouth moves to speak. It's no wonder she doesn't recognize me; my face likely looks as bad as I feel.

She throws herself at me again and I dart away just in time. She stumbles into the fence. After pulling herself up, she comes at me again, screaming insults the whole way. She isn't going to stop unless I force her to stop. I turn, looking for a way out of this mess. The few prisoners left in the courtyard look our way, watching Ava's fight. They spot me in my guard uniform and they begin jogging toward us. They're still a good way off, but it won't take them long to reach me.

My adrenaline goes into overtime, hammering though my veins. I have to think fast.

She lunges again and the other prisoners draw closer.

This cannot be happening. I can't hurt Ava. I can't. Hot tears burn my eyes and my throat swells.

A small boulder lays half-buried in the grass. Getting away from her would be easy. All I have to do is hit her with it, but I can't do it. It's Ava. She's my friend. She was unfortunate enough to get caught in the Greater's trap just like me.

Tears stream down my face. "Ava, stop. Please!"

She lunges again, this time scratching my already tender face.

The prisoners are a few yards away now, but I can't get around Ava to get away from them.

God help me.

I lunge for the rock and spin around quickly. The rock makes a terrible, sickening, earth-shattering thud when it connects with her skull. Her eyes roll back and she falls to the ground. I leap over her body as I run, and I pray she's OK as I bolt through the high grass toward the bridge. The guards in the trucks won't know I'm any different from the other guards. If I can get close enough to them to get away from the prisoners, then I might have a shot.

As I race across the front of the prison, I'm separated from the others by the fence rows that are still standing. Injured guards are already being loaded into the transport trucks that have arrived. As I near the gate a thought hits me. What if the warden communicated the reason for the riot? What if Supreme Moon has already discovered I was on this transport and the new guards are looking for me?

Glancing behind me, I see the prisoners have stopped following me. It was easy enough to see I was leading them straight toward the reinforcements.

I pause, my hands on my knees, gulping in fresh breaths of air. There has to be another way.

A truck engine rumbles to life and drives out of the courtyard, heading for the gate. A second one follows shortly. I squint through the fences. The driver of the second truck looks familiar, even with my exhausted eyes.

It's Guard Nev.

My legs kick into action and I dash for the gate. I have to get there in time for Guard Nev to see me. If he didn't get flagged yet, then I most likely haven't been either.

I reach the gate only moments before the second truck, waving my hands over my head. The truck slows and I race across the road to get in on the driver's side. Guard Nev opens the door and reaches his hand out to help me.

Another leap and I'll be on my way to getting out of here. I take a deep breath and lunge.

42

Guard Nev grabs my arm at the same time I leap onto the rumbling truck. "Move it!" he shouts.

I scramble over him and take the passenger seat, and he speeds across the bridge.

Screams and shouts carry on the wind, as does the sound of gun shots and explosions. I can't resist taking one last look at Lesser City 5—the prison. The scene behind me is chaos, and I almost feel like Lot's wife when I read the Old Testament story in the book of Genesis. She turned into a pillar of salt. Thankfully, I'm still me.

"They'll be coming for you. They'll probably be there when you reach home. You shouldn't go there."

"I have to!" I say. "I have to get my things." My Bible, but especially Mom's perfume. That is more important to me than ever. I shudder when I realize I almost left them behind.

Guard Nev shakes his head. "Nothing is worth getting caught over. Once we're across the bridge we have to go west."

"I have to try."

He doesn't like it, but he agrees to drop me off at the edge of the city so I can make my way home. "Don't forget about the scanners. If they pinpoint your location, they'll be on you in seconds. Once you get what you need, you have to run. Stay hidden and go west. I'll find you."

I nod, my heart pounding out of control. What have I gotten myself into? "Goodbye, Guard Nev. Thank you for being my friend."

He doesn't smile or nod. "I owe you much more than you owe me. Miriam taught me a lot in my time with her. Thank you."

In spite of the hell around us, a smile moves over my face. Guard Nev believes in God. Maybe I'm not as worthless as I think.

I squeeze his hand, then jump from the truck. It speeds away from the city, headed who knows where.

People stand on the streets, staring. They're not looking at me, though—they stare across the water.

I use their distraction to run.

Kassy's help in learning the city streets is definitely coming in handy now. I race through alleyways, trying to keep my mind from wandering.

Fischer. My heart aches. How could we leave him behind? What will happen to him?

God, why? Why let me find him just to take him away again?

I put the thoughts away for later as I near home. I reach my apartment and sneak in the back door. Someone may have seen me by now, but I can be quick at this point.

My nerves calm as I take the steps two at a time, all the way to the seventh floor. I gasp for breath as I make it to my landing, but I stop cold when I see the doorman outside my door.

He takes in my appearance and frowns. "Are you alright, Miss?"

I wait for guards to storm the hallway, but none show up. The doorman doesn't seem to realize I'm in big trouble.

"This letter came for you," he says, holding out an envelope. He watches me curiously.

I swallow hard, my breathing steadying. "Thank you." I take the letter.

He backs away and I push into my apartment. Two things. All I need are two things. I stumble toward the bathroom.

"No." The word escapes in a breathless whisper.

The hair dryer has been ripped from the wall, and the Bible is gone. I'm so thankful that I destroyed Keegan's letters. They would have found them all.

A letter! I rip open the envelope the doorman gave me and read the single line.

K said to tell you "he believes." Whatever that means. ~L

Lilith. She agreed to help us one last time after all. And Keegan? He believes! It's one last tiny ray of light in this vastly bleak day.

Sobs choke me and I grip the wall as I walk to my night stand. I'm not sure if I cry happy tears over Keegan or simply tears of pure frustration. I reach the night stand and run my hand through the drawer. It's empty. I jerk it off the tracks and turn it upside down. It has to be here!

But it's not.

"No," I say again, falling to my knees and crying. Mom's perfume is gone. They've taken everything from me.

Everything.

I curl into a ball and don't fight the tears that dampen the carpet. These are not happy tears after all. A few minutes pass and someone enters the apartment. Footsteps stomp across the floor, and strong arms pull me to a standing position. Someone slips cuffs onto my wrists and drags me into the hall. Amazingly, they take me down the stairs and quietly out the back, to a long transporter in the alley. Supreme Moon's transporter. They must want to keep the drama to a minimum.

Of course. They don't want everyone to know of the "dissention" taking place right in their own city.

The guard pushes me inside and the transporter drives away.

My mind screams at me to remove the cuffs, to fight, but I have nothing left to give.

I assume we're going to the Mansion, but we take a different turn. I recognize the medical center from my second day here, the day they ran the new tests.

At the center, the guard takes me inside, leading me by an arm. Supreme Moon paces the room, and once I'm in the auditorium he takes hold of me and shoves me toward the same table I lay on before. His eyes spew hatred and his face is an unhealthy shade of red. He says nothing as he straps me down.

The cloth cuts into my raw skin and I grunt, but he makes no notice.

"Put it in her vein," Supreme Moon commands.

A medic moves forward and sticks a long needle into my arm. I bite back a gasp of pain.

"What are you doing?" I ask, finally unable to sit by and watch my own torture.

Supreme Moon snarls at me but doesn't answer my question.

The medic places small, metal probes on either side of my head. The screens on the wall flash to life.

It only takes a moment for the medicine pumping into my body to take effect. My mind begins drifting just as I realize what's happening. Supreme Moon wants answers, and he's going after them right now.

I want to cry...and then I want nothing.

                                                  ॐ

I wake up in a transporter outside of the mansion. A different guard is there to pull me out and march me inside. This one is a woman, and she's not nearly as gentle as the guard at the apartment. She shoves me up the steps and I fall, scratching my knee. I haven't fully gotten my bearings from being drugged, and my balance is still off.

"Get up," she growls.

I scramble to my feet and hurry inside.

Supreme Moon waits in his study. I've never seen this part of his home before. It is dark, almost completely black.

"Sit," he commands.

I obey.

"I am demoting you today. You will leave Greater City immediately. You will never see your friends or family again, and you will die a Lesser—with none of the help you wanted to offer them. And you know what else? I'm glad your mother is dead. She was a fool and I shouldn't have ever trusted her to begin with."

My resolve returns like a flash of angry lightning. "You can never kill the message I spread. People want freedom, and they deserve to have it."

He sneers. "You and your silly beliefs. You know nothing—you think you do, but you don't. You know about the prison, that the people were being shipped away, but do you know where?"

No.

He stomps over to me and slaps me hard across

the face.

My head whips back and my thoughts swirl.

"Of course you don't know. You told me so only an hour ago in your dreams. It turns out you know almost nothing—but the things you do know? I will take care of that soon."

Hot oil ripples down my back and I cringe. Miriam and her people are no longer safe, because of me. I must have told Supreme Moon everything he wanted to know—about Fischer, about Guard Nev, about the Free. What else does he know?

It can't really matter. Not now.

His eyes blaze with a madness I've never seen before. He paces the floor like a crazed man, his words tumbling out in a barely discernible ramble.

"They found it easy to take over after everything had been destroyed. At first they didn't ask for much— only our men as soldiers. But after a while, they wanted more."

Who? I have no idea what he's talking about.

"By then the people had become so used to violence and harsh living conditions that it was easy to make the transition. The enemy moved in and took control of the people. They had a few requirements for allowing us to live, though. We would provide goods for trade, and we wouldn't promote anything that could cause dissention."

I realize he's talking about the past—about the beginning of our society.

So that's why we have outlying cities and religion is outlawed. This must have been the event Miriam talked about.

"We are not our own, Hana Norfolk." His words pull me back to the here and now. "We have a mother country, and we must follow her rules only."

Supreme Moon scowls at me and I wince, afraid he'll hit me again, but he doesn't. "You have allowed religion to spread, and you have taken away their soldiers. You have obliterated two of their three rules."

"There will be retribution," he goes on. I catch it then, the slight catch in his voice. A warble. A fear.

Whoever this mother country is, this enemy, they are powerful.

He stands nose to nose with me now, his cold eyes boring into mine. "I hope that when it comes, you are the first to die."

I had no idea. None of us had any idea, did we?

But Guard Nev knew. This is why he always tried to stop me. But something else Supreme Moon said sticks out to me: He was a fool to trust my mother.

Tears burn in my eyes and throat, and a million questions race through my mind.

How does he know my mother? How many died in the riots? Where will the people go now? Was Fischer caught? What will they do to Keegan?

But I keep quiet. Supreme Moon will only use the answers to torment me.

"You may have noble ideas about becoming Lesser. You may think you will be allowed to train them now, to teach them how to live, but you won't. You won't be able to do anything with them, because where I'm sending you? You won't last a week."

He motions for someone to take me away, and a guard materializes from behind a doorway. The guard takes me by the arms and drags me from the room, down another dark hallway and down a dim flight of stairs. We must be in the basement of the mansion, but as my eyes adjust to the light, I realize it's no ordinary basement. It's a dungeon; the kind I thought only existed in story books.

I'm shoved into a cell and the metal doors clang shut behind me. How long will they keep me here? Will I be fed? Given water? Allowed to use the restroom?

Be still and know that I am God.

The words are familiar, but how can I believe? I sit in a prison cell, and I'm about to be demoted. They are sending me to Lesser City 4. I am sure of it.

What kind of people are the people of Lesser 4? What will they do to me?

I remember God's whispers to me, and I close my eyes. I can do this. With God's help I can do anything, even face an angry mother country. God is here, even in the darkness.

I pray. I don't know how long I sit alone, but I pray.

Finally, I take a deep, shaky breath and open my eyes. The dimness doesn't bother me now.

It is time to wait. My new life will begin, but my old life will not end. I will tell others God's message. I will do all I can to find anyone who made it out of the prison riot alive. I will get out of Lesser 4.

I will find deliverance, and then I will spread it.

Don't miss the rest of the ENSLAVED series

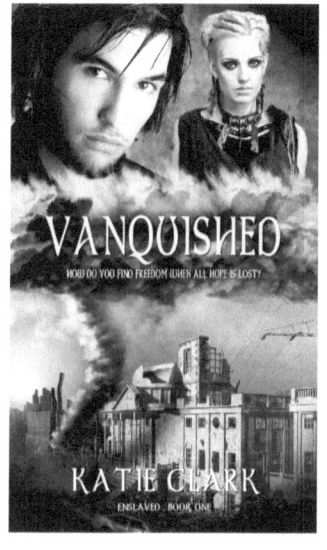

*How do You Find Freedom
When all Hope is Lost?*

VANQUISHED,
Book One

When Hana's mom is
diagnosed with the
mutation, she confesses to
Hana she doesn't know
what will happen if she dies.
Fischer, a medic at the
hospital, implies there is
Someone who can help–but
religion's been outlawed.

Hana embarks on a dangerous journey, seeking the
answers Fischer insists are available. But when the
truth is uncovered, will Hana stick to what she's been
taught? Or will she join the rebellion and take a stand
against an oppressive society?

Freedom is Within Reach, but is it at too High a Cost

REDEEMER,
Book Three

In this final chapter of the Enslaved series, Hana is faced not only with a new life, but an entirely new way of thinking. Unexpected friends give insight into who the Greaters truly are. Deciding what to do with this information sends Hana on what may be her very last journey. Ever.

Watch the book video:
http://youtu.be/e1q3Fg06I0A

Thank you for purchasing this Watershed Books title.
For other inspirational stories, please visit our on-line
bookstore at www.pelicanbookgroup.com.

For questions or more information, contact us at
customer@pelicanbookgroup.com.

Watershed Books
Make a Splash!™
an imprint of Pelican Ventures Book Group
www.PelicanBookGroup.com

Connect with Us
www.facebook.com/Pelicanbookgroup
www.twitter.com/pelicanbookgrp

To receive news and specials, subscribe to our bulletin
http://pelink.us/bulletin

May God's glory shine through
this inspirational work of fiction.

AMDG

www.ingramcontent.com/pod-product-compliance
Lightning Source LLC
Chambersburg PA
CBHW050403260626
47156CB00003B/857